CREEPY CLASSICS III

CREEPY CLASSICS III

*More hair-raising
horror from the masters
of the macabre*

compiled and edited by

Glen and Karen Bledsoe

ROXBURY PARK

Lowell House

C L A S S I C S

NTC/Contemporary Publishing Group

Published by Lowell House
A division of NTC/Contemporary Publishing Group, Inc.
4255 West Touhy Avenue, Lincolnwood (Chicago), Illinois 60712-1975
U.S.A.

Lowell House books can be purchased at special discounts when ordered in bulk for premiums and special sales. Contact Department CS at the following address:

NTC/Contemporary Publishing Group
4255 West Touhy Avenue
Lincolnwood, IL 60712-1975
1-800-323-4900

ISBN: 0-7373-9856-6
Library of Congress Catalog Card Number: 98-67905

Roxbury Park is a division of NTC/Contemporary Publishing Group, Inc.

Managing Director and Publisher: Jack Artenstein
Editor in Chief, Roxbury Park Books: Michael Artenstein
Director of Publishing Services: Rena Copperman

Printed and bound in the United States of America
00 01 02 DHD 10 9 8 7 6 5 4 3 2

CONTENTS

INTRODUCTION

Your reading tastes have now matured to the point where you realize that for a story to be scary, for it to be entertaining in that special, deliciously horrible way, it does not need to be (and shouldn't be) unnecessarily violent—popping eyeballs, chainsaws, dripping gore, and all that cheap rubbish. Tales that truly give you the creeps do so with original stories, clever plot twists, vivid language, and uncommon imagination. Good! I am glad you agree. Then this is the book for you.

These stories were written by masters of the late 19th- and early 20th-century fiction. A few of their names may be familiar, but some surely won't be. Those writers who have been all but forgotten today are, perhaps, the most interesting discoveries. Take William Hope Hodgson, for instance. There are more of his Carnacki stories, but not many. Savor each one you find, for there is nothing else quite like them. You've probably heard of Sir Arthur Conan Doyle, the creator of Sherlock Holmes, but did you know he also wrote tales of mystery and terror? Not to forget F. Marion Crawford's "The Screaming Skull," one of the most nerve-wracking stories ever written—a fine piece for a stormy evening alone.

There are two other stories, a total of five. But you don't want to know too much about what awaits you, do you? You understand that for your skin to creep, for your scalp to prickle, for your stomach to begin to be sweet and queasy at the same time, there must be some element of surprise.

Welcome to *Creepy Classics III*. May you find these masters of classic horror to your taste.

THE WHISTLING ROOM (1912)

by

William Hope Hodgson

(1877–1918)

William Hope Hodgson *had an imagination as rich as any writer of his generation. The author of "The Night Land," "The House of the Border" and "The Boats of Glen Carrig," Hodgson also wrote a series of short stories about a character named only Carnacki. Like Algernon Blackwood's John Silence and Seabury Quinn's Jules de Grandin, Carnacki hunted ghosts and probed into supernatural occurrences.*

The stories are told in an unusual way. Oddly enough, although Carnacki is an adventurer in the mold of Indiana Jones, we never really actually see him do anything. He calls together a group of friends—including the narrator of the story, who remains nameless—and then, story after story, enthusiastically relates his encounters with the unearthly. But these stories are not just about an interesting character. The tales build, and before the end one finds out exactly why Hodgson deserves his reputation for imaginative storytelling.

CARNACKI SHOOK A FRIENDLY FIST AT ME AS I ENTERED late. Then he opened the door into the dining room and ushered the four of us—Jessop, Arkright, Taylor, and myself—into dinner.

We dined well, as usual, and, equally as usual, Carnacki was pretty silent during the meal. At the end we took our wine and cigars to our usual positions, and Carnacki—having

1

got himself comfortable in his big chair—began without any preliminary:

"I have just got back from Ireland again," he said. "And I thought you chaps would be interested to hear my news. Besides, I fancy I shall see the thing clearer after I have told it all out straight. I must tell you this though, from the beginning up to the present moment I have been utterly and completely stumped. I have stumbled upon one of the most peculiar cases of haunting—or devilment of some sort—that I have come against. Now listen.

"I have been spending the last few weeks at Arlestrae Castle, about 20 miles northeast of Galway. I got a letter about a month ago from a Mr. Sid K. Tassoc, who it seemed had bought the place lately and moved in only to find that he had bought a very peculiar piece of property.

"When I got there, he met me at the station, driving a jaunting car and drove me up to the castle. I found that he was pigging it there with his boy brother and another American who seemed to be half-servant and half-companion. It seems that all the servants had left the place, in a body as you might say; and now they were managing among themselves assisted by some day help.

"The three of them got together a scratch feed, and Tassoc told me all about the trouble while we were at table. It is most extraordinary and different from anything that I have had to do with; though that Buzzing case was very odd, too.

"Tassoc began right in the middle of his story. 'We've got a room in this shanty,' he said, 'which has got a most infernal whistling in it, sort of haunting it. The thing starts any time—you never know when—and it goes on until it frightens you. All the servants have gone, as you know. It's not ordinary whistling, and it isn't the wind. Wait till you hear it.'

" 'We're all carrying guns,' the boy said and slapped his coat pocket.

" 'As bad as that?' I said.

"The older boy nodded. 'It may be soft,' he replied, 'but wait till you've heard it. Sometimes I think it's some infernal thing, and the next moment I'm just as sure that someone's playing a trick on me.'

" 'Why?' I asked. 'What is to be gained?'

" 'You mean,' he said, 'that people usually have some good reason for playing tricks as elaborate as this. Well, I'll tell you. There's a lady in this province by the name of Miss Donnehue who's going to be my wife in two months. She's as pretty as they come, and so far as I can see I've just stuck my head into an Irish hornet's nest. There's about two dozen hot young Irishmen who've been courting her for the last two years, and now that I've come along and cut them out they're feeling raw against me. Do you begin to understand the possibilities?'

" 'Yes,' I said. 'Perhaps I do in a vague sort of way, but I don't see how all this affects the room?'

" 'Like this,' he said. 'When I'd fixed it up with Miss Donnehue, I looked out for a place and bought this little house shanty. Afterward I told her—one evening during dinner—that I'd decided to tie up here. And then she asked me whether I wasn't afraid of the whistling room. I told her it must have been thrown in gratis, as I'd heard nothing about it. There were some of her men friends present, and I saw a smile go round. I found out, after a bit of questioning, that several people have bought this place during the last 20-odd years. And it was always on the market again, after a trial.

" 'Well, the chaps started to bait me a bit, and offered to take bets after dinner that I'd not stay six months in the place. I looked once or twice to Miss Donnehue so as to see if

3

they were pulling my leg, but I could see that she didn't take it as a joke at all. Partly, I think, because there was a bit of a sneer in the way the men were heckling me, and partly because she really believes there is something in this yarn of the whistling room.

" 'However, after dinner I did what I could to even things up with the others. I nailed all their bets and screwed them down hard and safe. I guess some of them are going to be hard hit, unless I lose—which I don't mean to. Well, there you have practically the whole yarn.'

" 'Not quite,' I told him. 'All that I know is that you have bought a castle with a room in it that is in some way strange, and that you've been doing some betting. Also, I know that your servants have got frightened and run away. Tell me something about the whistling?'

" 'Oh that,' said Tassoc. 'That started the second night we were in. I'd had a good look round the room, in the daytime as you can understand; for the talk up at Arlestrae— Miss Donnehue's place—had made me wonder a bit. But it seems just as usual as some of the other rooms in the old wing, only perhaps a bit more lonesome. But that may be only because of the talk about it, you know.

" 'The whistling started about ten o'clock on the second night, as I said. Tom and I were in the library when we heard an awfully weird whistling coming along the east corridor—the room is in the east wing, you know.

" 'That's that blessed ghost!' I said to Tom, and we grabbed the lamps off the table, and went up to have a look. I tell you, even as we ran along the corridor, it took me a bit in the throat; it was so beastly strange. It was a sort of tune in a way, but more as if a devil or some rotten thing were laughing at you and going to get round at your back. That's how it makes you feel.

" 'When we got to the door we didn't wait, but rushed it open. And then I tell you the sound of the thing fairly hit me in the face. Tom said he got it the same way—sort of felt stunned and bewildered. We looked all round and soon got so nervous, we just cleared out, and I locked the door.

" 'We came down here and had a stiff drink each. Then we got fit again and began to think we'd been nicely had. So we took sticks and went out into the grounds, thinking after all it must be some of these confounded Irishmen working the ghost trick on us. But there was not a leg stirring.

" 'We went back into the house, walked over it, and then paid another visit to the room. But we simply couldn't stand it. We fairly ran out and locked the door again. I don't know how to put it into words, but I had a feeling of being up against something that was rottenly dangerous. You know! We've carried our guns ever since.

" 'Of course, we searched the room the next day and the whole house place. We even hunted round the grounds, but there was nothing unusual. And now I don't know what to think except that the sensible part of me tells me that it's some plan of these wild Irishmen to try to get a rise out of me.'

" 'Done anything since?' I asked him.

" 'Yes,' he said, 'watched outside of the door of the room at night, and chased round the grounds, and sounded the walls and floor of the room. We've done everything we could think of, and it's beginning to get on our nerves. So we sent for you.'

"By this we had finished eating. As we rose from the table Tassoc suddenly called out: 'Ssh!'

"We were instantly silent, listening. Then I heard it, an extraordinary hooning whistle, monstrous and inhuman, coming from far away through corridors to my right.

"'By God!' said Tassoc, 'and it's scarcely dark yet! Grab those candles, both of you, and come along.'

"In a few moments we were all out of the door and racing up the stairs. Tassoc turned into a long corridor and we followed, shielding our candles as we ran. The sound seemed to fill all the passage as we drew near until I had the feeling that the whole air throbbed under the power of some wanton immense force—a sense of an actual taint, as you might say, of monstrosity all about us.

"Tassoc unlocked the door. Then, giving it a push with his foot, jumped back, and drew his revolver. As the door flew open the sound beat out at us with an effect impossible to explain to one who has not heard it—with a certain, horrible personal note in it; as if in there in the darkness you could picture the room rocking and creaking in a mad, vile glee to its own filthy piping and whistling and hooning. To stand there and listen was to be stunned by realization. It was as if someone showed you the mouth of a vast pit suddenly and said: That's hell. And you knew that they had spoken the truth. Do you get it, even a little bit?

"I stepped back a pace into the room, held the candle over my head, and looked quickly round. Tassoc and his brother joined me. The man came up at the back, and we all held our candles high. I was deafened with the shrill, piping hoon of the whistling. And then, clear in my ear, something seemed to be saying to me: 'Get out of here—quick! Quick! Quick!'

"As you chaps know, I never neglect that sort of thing. Sometimes it may be nothing but nerves, but as you will remember it was just such a warning that saved me in the Gray Dog case and in the Yellow Finger experiments as well as other times. Well, I turned sharp round to the others: 'Out!' I said. 'For God's sake, out quick.' And in an instant I had them into the passage.

"There came an extraordinary yelling scream into the hideous whistling, and then, like a clap of thunder, an utter silence. I slammed the door and locked it. Then, taking the key, I looked round at the others. They were pretty white, and I imagine I must have looked that way too. And there we stood a moment, silent.

" 'Come down out of this and have some whisky,' said Tassoc, at last, in a voice he tried to make ordinary, and he led the way. I was the back man, and I know we all kept looking over our shoulders. When we got downstairs, Tassoc passed the bottle round. He took a drink himself and slapped his glass down on to the table. Then sat down with a thud.

" 'That's a lovely thing to have in the house with you, isn't it?' he said. And directly afterward: 'What on earth made you hustle us all out like that, Carnacki?'

" 'Something seemed to be telling me to get out, quick,' I said. 'Sounds a bit silly-superstitious, I know. But when you are meddling with this sort of thing, you've got to take notice of strange fancies and risk being laughed at.'

"I told him then about the Gray Dog business, and he nodded a lot to that. 'Of course,' I said, 'this may be nothing more than those would-be rivals of yours playing some funny game; but personally though I'm going to keep an open mind, I feel that there is something beastly and dangerous about this thing.'

"We talked for a while longer, and then Tassoc suggested billiards, which we played in a pretty halfhearted fashion and all the time cocking an ear to the door, as you might say, for sounds. But none came, and later after coffee he suggested early bed and a thorough overhaul of the room on the morrow.

"My bedroom was in the newer part of the castle, and the door opened into the picture gallery. At the east end of

7

the gallery was the entrance to the corridor of the east wing. This was shut off from the gallery by two old and heavy oak doors, which looked rather odd and quaint beside the more modern doors of the various rooms.

"When I reached my room I did not go to bed, but began to unpack my instrument-trunk of which I had retained the key. I intended to take one or two preliminary steps at once in my investigation of the extraordinary whistling.

"Presently, when the castle had settled into quietness, I slipped out of my room and across to the entrance of the great corridor. I opened one of the low, squat doors and threw the beam of my pocket searchlight down the passage. It was empty, and I went through the doorway and pushed-to the oak door behind me. Then along the great passageway throwing my light before and behind and keeping my revolver handy.

"I had hung a protection belt of garlic round my neck, and the smell of it seemed to fill the corridor and give me assurance for, as you all know, it is a wonderful protection against the more usual forms of semimaterialization by which I supposed the whistling might be produced; though, at that period of my investigation, I was quite prepared to find it due to some perfectly natural cause, for it is astonishing the enormous number of cases that prove to have nothing abnormal in them.

"In addition to wearing the necklet, I had plugged my ears loosely with garlic, and as I did not intend to stay more than a few minutes in the room, I hoped to be safe.

"When I reached the door and put my hand into my pocket for the key, I had a sudden feeling of sickening funk. But I was not going to back out if I could help it. I unlocked the door and turned the handle. Then I gave the door a sharp push with my foot as Tassoc had done and drew my revolver, though I did not expect to have any use for it, really.

"I shone the searchlight all round the room and then stepped inside with a disgustingly horrible feeling of walking slap into a waiting danger. I stood a few seconds, waiting, and nothing happened. The empty room showed bare from corner to corner. And then, you know, I realized that the room was full of an abominable silence; can you understand that? A sort of purposeful silence, just as sickening as any of the filthy noises the things have power to make. Do you remember what I told you about that Silent Garden business? Well, this room had just that same malevolent silence—the beastly quietness of a thing that is looking at you and not seeable itself and thinks that it has got you. Oh, I recognized it instantly, and I whipped the top off my lantern so as to have light over the whole room.

"Then I set to, working like fury and keeping my glance all about me. I sealed the two windows with lengths of human hair, right across, and sealed them at every frame. As I worked, an odd, scarcely perceptible tenseness stole into the air of the place, and the silence seemed, if you can understand me, to grow more solid. I knew then that I had no business there without full protection.

"I finished the window and hurried over to the great fireplace. This is a huge affair, and has an odd gallows iron, I think they are called, projecting from the back of the arch. I sealed the opening with seven human hairs—the seventh crossing the six others.

"Then, just as I was making an end, a low, mocking whistle grew in the room. A cold, nervous pricking went up my spine and round my forehead from the back. The hideous

sound filled all the room with an extraordinary, grotesque parody of human whistling, too gigantic to be human—as if something gargantuan and monstrous made the sounds softly. As I stood there a last moment, pressing down the final seal, I had no doubt but that I had come across one of those rare and horrible cases of the inanimate reproducing the functions of the animate. I made a grab for my lamp and went quickly to the door, looking over my shoulder and listening for the thing that I expected. It came, just as I got my hand upon the handle—a squeal of incredible, malevolent anger, piercing through the low hooning of the whistling. I dashed out, slamming the door and locking it. I leant a little against the opposite wall of the corridor, feeling rather funny; for it had been a narrow squeak. . . . 'There be no safety to be gained by guards of holiness when the monster hath pow'r to speak through woode and stone.' So runs the passage in the Sigsand manuscript, and I proved it in that Nodding Door business. There is no protection against this particular form of monster, except possibly for a fractional period of time; for it can reproduce itself in or take to its purpose, the very protective material which you may use and has the power to 'forme within the pentacle'; though not immediately. There is, of course, the possibility of the unknown last line of the Saaamaaa ritual being uttered; but it is too uncertain to count upon, and the danger is too hideous. And even then it has no power to protect for more than 'maybee five beats of the hearte,' as the Sigsand has it.

"Inside of the room, there was now a constant, meditative, hooning whistling; but presently this ceased, and the silence seemed worse, for there is such a sense of hidden mischief in a silence.

"After a little, I sealed the door with crossed hairs and then cleared off down the great passage and so to bed.

"For a long time I lay awake, but managed eventually to get some sleep. Yet, about two o'clock I was waked by the hooning whistling of the room coming to me even through the closed doors. The sound was tremendous and seemed to beat through the whole house with a presiding sense of terror. As if (I remember thinking) some monstrous giant had been holding a mad carnival with itself at the end of that great passage.

"I got up and sat on the edge of the bed, wondering whether to go along and have a look at the seal, and suddenly there came a thump on my door. Tassoc walked in with his dressing gown over his pajamas.

"'I thought it would have waked you, so I came along to have a talk,' he said. 'I can't sleep. Beautiful! Isn't it!'

"'Extraordinary!' I said and tossed him my case.

"He lit a cigarette, and we sat and talked for about an hour; and all the time that noise went on down at the end of the big corridor.

"Suddenly, Tassoc stood up:

"'Let's take our guns and go and examine the brute,' he said and turned toward the door.

"'No!' I said. 'By Jove—No! I can't say anything definite yet, but I believe that room is about as dangerous as it well can be.'

"'Haunted—really haunted?' he asked, keenly and without any of his frequent banter.

"I told him, of course, that I could not say a definite yes or no to such a question, but that I hoped to be able to make a statement soon. Then I gave him a little lecture on the false rematerialization of the animate force through the inanimate inert. He began then to see the particular way in which the room might be dangerous, if it were really the subject of a manifestation.

"About an hour later, the whistling ceased quite suddenly, and Tassoc went off again to bed. I went back to mine, also, and eventually got another spell of sleep.

"In the morning, I went along to the room. I found the seals on the door intact. Then I went in. The window seals and the hair were all right, but the seventh hair across the great fireplace was broken. This set me thinking. I knew that it might, very possibly, have snapped through my having tensioned it too highly, but then again it might have been broken by something else. Yet it was scarcely possible that a man, for instance, could have passed between the six unbroken hairs; for no one would ever have noticed them entering the room that way, you see, but just walked through them ignorant of their very existence.

"I removed the other hairs and the seals. Then I looked up the chimney. It went up straight, and I could see blue sky at the top. It was a big, open flue, and free from any suggestion of hiding places or corners. Yet of course, I did not trust to any such casual examination, and after breakfast I put on my overalls and climbed to the very top, sounding all the way; but I found nothing.

"Then I came down and went over the whole of the room—floor, ceiling, and walls, mapping them out in six-inch squares and sounding with both hammer and probe. But there was nothing abnormal.

"Afterward, I made a three-week search of the whole castle in the same thorough way, but found nothing. I went even further then, for at night when the whistling commenced, I made a microphone test. You see, if the whistling were mechanically produced, this test would have made evident to me the working of the machinery if there were any such concealed within the walls. It certainly was an up-to-date method of examination, as you must allow.

13

"Of course, I did not think that any of Tassoc's rivals had fixed up any mechanical contrivance, but I thought it just possible that there had been some such thing for producing the whistling, made away back in the years perhaps with the intention of giving the room a reputation that would ensure its being free of inquisitive folk. You see what I mean? Well, of course, it was just possible, if this were the case, that someone knew the secret of the machinery and was utilizing the knowledge to play this devil of a prank on Tassoc. The microphone test of the walls would certainly have made this known to me, as I have said; but there was nothing of the sort in the castle; so that I had practically no doubt at all now, but that it was a genuine case of what is popularly termed 'haunting.'

"All this time every night, and sometimes most of each night, the hooning whistling of the room was intolerable. It was as if an intelligence there knew that steps were being taken against it and piped and hooned in a sort of mad, mocking contempt. I tell you, it was as extraordinary as it was horrible. Time after time, I went along—tiptoeing noiselessly on stockinged feet—to the sealed door (for I always kept the room sealed). I went at all hours of the night and often the whistling inside would seem to change to a brutally malignant note, as though the half-animate monster saw me plainly through the shut door. And all the time the shrieking, hooning whistling would fill the whole corridor so that I used to feel a precious lonely chap, messing about there with one of hell's mysteries.

"And every morning, I would enter the room and examine the different hairs and seals. You see, after the first week, I had stretched parallel hairs all along the walls of the room and along the ceiling, but over the floor which was of polished stone I had set out little, colorless wafers, tacky side uppermost. Each wafer was numbered, and they were arranged after a definite plan so that I should be able to trace the exact movements of any living thing that went across the floor.

"You will see that no material being or creature could possibly have entered that room without leaving many signs to tell me about it. But nothing was ever disturbed, and I began to think that I should have to risk an attempt to stay the night in the room in the electric pentacle. Yet, mind you, I knew that it would be a crazy thing to do, but I was getting stumped and ready to do anything.

"Once about midnight, I did break the seal on the door and have a quick look in; but, I tell you, the whole room gave one mad yell and seemed to come toward me in a great belly of shadows—as if the walls had bellied in toward me. Of course, that must have been fancy. Anyway, the yell was sufficient, and I slammed the door and locked it, feeling a bit weak down my spine. You know the feeling.

"And then when I had got to that state of readiness for anything, I made something of a discovery. It was about one in the morning, and I was walking slowly round the castle keeping in the soft grass. I had come under the shadow of the east front, and far above me I could hear the vile, hooning whistle of the room, up in the darkness of the unlit wing. Then, suddenly, a little in front of me, I heard a man's voice, speaking low, but evidently in glee:

"'By george! You chaps, but I wouldn't care to bring a wife home in that!' it said, in the tone of the cultured Irish.

"Someone started to reply; but there came a sharp exclamation, and then a rush, and I heard footsteps running in all directions. Evidently, the men had spotted me.

"For a few seconds, I stood there, feeling awful. After all, they were at the bottom of the haunting! Do you see what a big fool it made me seem? I had no doubt but that they were some of Tassoc's rivals; and here I had been feeling in every bone that I had hit a real, bad, genuine case! And then, you know, there came the memory of hundreds of details that made me just as much in doubt again. Anyway, whether it was natural or ab-natural, there was a great deal yet to be cleared up.

"I told Tassoc next morning what I had discovered, and through the whole of every night, for five nights we kept a close watch round the east wing; but there was never a sign of anyone prowling about. And all the time, almost from evening to dawn, that grotesque whistling would hoon incredibly, far above us in the darkness.

"On the morning after the fifth night, I received a wire from here which brought me home by the next boat. I explained to Tassoc that I was simply bound to come away for a few days, but told him to keep up the watch round the castle. One thing I was very careful to do and that was to make him absolutely promise never to go into the room between sunset and sunrise. I made it clear to him that we knew nothing definite yet, one way or the other; and if the room were what I had first thought it to be, it might be a lot better for him to die first than enter it after dark.

"When I got here and had finished my business, I thought you chaps would be interested; and also I wanted to get it all spread out clear in my mind, so I rung you up. I am going over again tomorrow, and when I get back I ought to have something pretty extraordinary to tell you. By the way, there is a curious thing I forgot to tell you. I tried to get a phonographic record of the whistling, but it simply produced no impression on the wax at all. That is one of the things that has made me feel strange, I can tell you. Another extraordinary thing is that the microphone will not magnify the sound—will not even transmit it, seems to take no account of it and acts as if it were nonexistent. I am absolutely and utterly stumped, up to the present. I am a wee bit curious to see whether any of your dear clever heads can make sense of it. I cannot—not yet."

He rose to his feet.

"Good night, all," he said and began to usher us out abruptly, but without offense, into the night.

A fortnight later he dropped each of us a card, and you can imagine that I was not late this time. When we arrived Carnacki took us straight into dinner, and when we had finished and all made ourselves comfortable, he began again where he had left off:

"Now just listen quietly for I have got something pretty curious to tell you. I got back late at night, and I had to walk up to the castle as I had not warned them that I was coming. It was bright moonlight so that the walk was rather a pleasure than otherwise. When I got there the whole place was in darkness, and I thought I would take a walk round outside to see whether Tassoc or his brother was keeping watch. But I could not find them anywhere and concluded that they had got tired of it and gone off to bed.

"As I returned across the front of the east wing I caught the hooning whistling of the room coming down strangely through the stillness of the night. It had a weird note in it, I remember—low and constant, oddly meditative. I looked up at the window, bright in the moonlight, and got a sudden thought to bring a ladder from the stable yard and try to get a look into the room through the window.

"With this notion I hunted round at the back of the castle among the straggle of offices and presently found a long, fairly light ladder—though it was heavy enough for one, goodness knows! And I thought at first that I should never get it reared. I managed at last and let the ends rest very quietly against the wall, a little below the sill of the larger window. Then, going silently, I went up the ladder.

Presently I had my face above the sill and was looking in alone with the moonlight.

"Of course, the curious whistling sounded louder up there, but it still conveyed that peculiar sense of something whistling quietly to itself—can you understand? Though, for all the meditative lowness of the note, the horrible, gargantuan quality was distinct—a mighty parody of the human as if I stood there and listened to the whistling from the lips of a monster with a man's soul.

"And then, you know, I saw something. The floor in the middle of the huge, empty room was puckered upward in the center into a strange soft-looking mound, parted at the top into an ever changing hole that pulsated to that great, gentle hooning. At times as I watched, I saw the heaving of the indented mound, gap across with a peculiar, inward suction as with the drawing of an enormous breath; then the thing would dilate and pout once more to the incredible melody. And suddenly as I stared, dumb, it came to me that the thing was living. I was looking at two enormous, blackened lips, blistered and brutal, there in the pale moonlight.

"Abruptly, they bulged out to a vast, pouting mound of force and sound, stiffened and swollen and hugely massive and clean-cut in the moonbeams. And a great sweat lay heavy on the vast upper lip. In the same moment of time, the whistling had burst into a mad screaming note that seemed to stun me even where I stood outside of the window. And then the following moment, I was staring blankly at the solid, undisturbed floor of the room—smooth, polished stone flooring from wall to wall, and there was an absolute silence.

"You can picture me staring into the quiet room and knowing what I knew. I felt like a sick, frightened kid and wanted to slide quietly down the ladder and run away. But in that very instant, I heard Tassoc's voice calling to me from within the room for help, help. My God! but I got such an awful dazed feeling, and I had a vague, bewildered notion that after all it was the Irishmen who had got him in there and were taking it out of him. And then the call came again, and I burst the window and jumped in to help him. I had a confused idea that the call had come from within the shadow of the great fireplace, and I raced across to it; but there was no one there.

"'Tassoc!' I shouted, and my voice went empty-sounding round the great apartment; and then in a flash, I knew that Tassoc had never called. I whirled round sick with fear toward the window, and as I did so a frightful, exultant whistling scream burst through the room. On my left, the end wall had bellied in toward me in a pair of gargantuan lips, black and utterly monstrous, to within a yard of my face. I fumbled for a mad instant at my revolver—not for it, but for myself, the danger was a thousand times worse than death. And then, suddenly, the unknown last line of the Saaamaaa ritual was whispered quite audibly in the room. Instantly, the thing happened that I have known once before. There came a sense as of dust falling continually and monotonously, and I knew that my life hung uncertain and suspended for a flash in a brief, reeling vertigo of unseeable things.

"Then that ended, and I knew that I might live. My soul and body blended again, and life and power came to me. I dashed furiously at the window and hurled myself out head-foremost; for I can tell you that I had stopped being afraid of death. I crashed down onto the ladder and slithered, grabbing and grabbing; and so came some way or other alive to the bottom. And there I sat in the soft, wet grass with the moonlight all about me; and far above, through the broken window of the room, there was a low whistling.

"That is the chief of it. I was not hurt, and I went round to the front and woke Tassoc up. When they let me in, we had a long yarn over some good whisky—for I was shaken to pieces—and I explained things as much as I could. I told Tassoc that the room would have to come down and every fragment of it burned in a blast furnace erected within a pentacle. He nodded. There was nothing to say. Then I went to bed.

"We turned a small army on to the work, and within 10 days that lovely thing had gone up in smoke, and what was left was calcined and clean.

"It was when the workmen were stripping the paneling that I got hold of a sound notion of the beginnings of that beastly development. Over the great fireplace after the great oak panels had been torn down, I found that there was let into the masonry a scrollwork of stone with on it an old inscription in ancient Celtic, that here in this room was burned Dian Tiansay, jester of King Alzof, who made the Song of Foolishness upon King Ernore of the Seventh Castle.

"When I got the translation clear, I gave it to Tassoc. He was tremendously excited, for he knew the old tale and took me down to the library to look at an old parchment that gave the story in detail. Afterward, I found that the incident was well known about the countryside, but always regarded more as a legend than as history. And no one seemed ever to have dreamt that the old east wing of Arlestrae Castle was the remains of the ancient Seventh Castle.

"From the old parchment I gathered that there had been a pretty dirty job done away back in the years. It seems that King Alzof and King Ernore had been enemies by birthright as you might say truly, but that nothing more than a little raiding had occurred on either side for years until Dian Tiansay made the Song of Foolishness upon King Ernore and sang it before King Alzof. So greatly was it appreciated that King Alzof gave the jester one of his ladies to wife.

"Presently, all the people of the land had come to know the song, and so it came at last to King Ernore, who was so angered that he made war upon his old enemy and took and burned him and his castle. But Dian Tiansay, the jester, he brought with him to his own place, and having torn his tongue out because of the song which he had made and sung, he imprisoned him in the room in the east wing (which was evidently used for unpleasant purposes), and the jester's wife he kept for himself having a fancy for her prettiness.

"But one night, Dian Tiansay's wife was not to be found, and in the morning they discovered her lying dead in her husband's arms, and he sitting, whistling the Song of Foolishness for he had no longer the power to sing it.

"Then they roasted Dian Tiansay in the great fireplace—probably from that self same galley iron which I have already mentioned. And until he died, Dian Tiansay ceased not to whistle the Song of Foolishness which he could no longer sing. But afterward 'in that room' there was often heard at night the sound of something whistling. And there 'grew a power in that room,' so that none dared to sleep in it. Presently, it would seem, the king went to another castle for the whistling troubled him.

"There you have it all. Of course, that is only a rough rendering of the translation of the parchment. But it sounds extraordinarily quaint. Don't you think so?"

"Yes," I said, answering for the lot. "But how did the thing grow to such a tremendous manifestation?"

"One of those cases of continuity of thought producing a positive action upon the immediate surrounding material," replied Carnacki. "The development must have been going forward through centuries to have produced such a monstrosity. It was a true instance of Saiitii manifestation, which I can best explain by likening it to a living spiritual fungus which involves the very structure of the ether-fiber itself, and of course in so doing, acquires an essential control over the material-substance involved in it. It is impossible to make it plainer in a few words."

"What broke the seventh hair?" asked Taylor.

But Carnacki did not know. He thought it was probably nothing but being too severely tensioned. He also explained that they found out that the men who had run away had not been up to mischief, but had come over secretly, merely to hear the whistling, which, indeed, had suddenly become the talk of the whole countryside.

"One other thing," said Arkright, "have you any idea what governs the use of the unknown last line of the Saaamaaa ritual? I know, of course, that it was used by the Ab-human priests in the Incantation of Raaaee; but what used it on your behalf, and what made it?"

"You had better read Harzan's monograph and my addenda to it, on astral coordination and interference," said Carnacki. "It is an extraordinary subject, and I can only say here that the human vibration may not be insulated from the astarral (as is always believed to be the case, in interferences by the ab-human) without immediate action being taken by those forces which govern the spinning of the outer circle. In other words, it is being proved, time after time, that there is some inscrutable protective force constantly intervening between the human soul (not the body, mind you,) and the outer monstrosities. Am I clear?"

"Yes, I think so," I replied. "And you believe that the room had become the material expression of the ancient jester—that his soul, rotten with hatred, had bred into a monster—eh?" I asked.

"Yes," said Carnacki, nodding, "I think you've put my thought rather neatly. It is an odd coincidence that Miss Donnehue is supposed to be descended (so I have heard since) from the same King Ernore. It makes one think some curious thoughts, doesn't it? The marriage coming on, and the room waking to fresh life. If she had gone into that room, ever . . . eh? It had waited a long time. Sins of the fathers. Yes, I've thought of that. They're to be married next week, and I am to be best man, which is a thing I hate. And he won his bets, rather! Just think, if ever she had gone into that room. Pretty horrible, eh?"

He nodded his head, grimly, and we four nodded back. Then he rose and took us collectively to the door and presently thrust us forth in friendly fashion on the embankment and into the fresh night air.

"Good night," we all called back and went to our various homes. If she had, eh? If she had? That is what I kept thinking.

THE MOONLIT ROAD (1893)

by
Ambrose Bierce
(1842–1913?)

Ambrose Gwinett Bierce, *a newspaperman, short story writer, Civil War soldier, and creator of The Devil's Dictionary, was known for his harsh and cynical wit.*

The following story from the collection "Can Such Things Be?" is told in three sections. The language is difficult and the vocabulary demanding, so please refer to the glossary at the end of the book or to a dictionary when the meaning of a word is so unclear that you can't understand the sentence. At first it's hard to see what these sections have to do with one another. Then, like pieces of a nightmare puzzle, they begin to fit together in a most gruesome, unexpected way.

Irony. The word is not used in this story, but it's what this tale is all about. The word irony has several shades of meaning, but for our purposes irony is an outcome of events that because of confusion or accident is contrary to what might have been expected.

Irony can be slightly humorous or sad. This story serves as an example of irony that is darkly bitter and with grim consequences.

1: STATEMENT OF JOEL HETMAN, JR.

I am the most unfortunate of men. Rich, respected, fairly well educated and of sound health—with many other advantages usually valued by those having them and coveted by those who have them not—I sometimes think that I should be less unhappy if they had been denied me, for then the contrast between my outer and my inner life would not be continually demanding a painful attention. In the stress of privation and

24

the need of effort I might sometimes forget the somber secret ever baffling the conjecture that it compels.

I am the only child of Joel and Julia Hetman. The one was a well-to-do country gentleman, the other a beautiful and accomplished woman to whom he was passionately attached with what I now know to have been a jealous and exacting devotion. The family home was a few miles from Nashville, Tennessee, a large, irregularly built dwelling of no particular order of architecture, a little way off the road, in a park of trees and shrubbery.

At the time of which I write I was 19 years old, a student at Yale. One day I received a telegram from my father of such urgency that in compliance with its unexplained demand, I left at once for home. At the railway station in Nashville a distant relative awaited me to apprise me of the reason for my recall: my mother had been barbarously murdered—why and by whom none could conjecture, but the circumstances were these.

My father had gone to Nashville, intending to return the next afternoon. Something prevented his accomplishing the business in hand, so he returned on the same night arriving just before the dawn. In his testimony before the coroner he explained that having no latchkey and not caring to disturb the sleeping servants, he had, with no clearly defined intention, gone round to the rear of the house. As he turned an angle of the building, he heard a sound as of a door gently closed and saw in the darkness, indistinctly, the figure of a man which instantly disappeared among the trees of the lawn. A hasty pursuit and brief search of the grounds in the belief that the trespasser was some one secretly visiting a servant proving fruitless, he entered at the unlocked door and mounted the stairs to my mother's chamber. Its door was open, and stepping into black darkness he fell headlong over some heavy object on the floor. I may spare myself the details; it was my poor mother, dead of strangulation by human hands!

Nothing had been taken from the house, the servants had heard no sound, and excepting those terrible finger marks upon the dead woman's throat—dear God! that I might forget them!—no trace of the assassin was ever found.

I gave up my studies and remained with my father who, naturally, was greatly changed. Always of a sedate, taciturn disposition, he now fell into so deep a dejection that nothing could hold his attention, yet anything—a footfall, the sudden closing of a door—aroused in him a fitful interest; one might have called it an apprehension. At any small surprise of the senses he would start visibly and sometimes turn pale, then relapse into a melancholy apathy deeper than before. I suppose he was what is called a "nervous wreck." As to me, I was younger then than now—there is much in that. Unacquainted with grief, I knew not how to appraise my bereavement; I could not rightly estimate the strength of the stroke.

One night, a few months after the dreadful event, my father and I walked home from the city. The full moon was about three hours above the eastern horizon; the entire countryside had the solemn stillness of a summer night; our footfalls and the ceaseless song of the katydids were the only sound. Black shadows of bordering trees lay athwart the road, which, in the short reaches between, gleamed a ghostly white. As we approached the gate to our dwelling whose front was in shadow, and in which no light shone, my father suddenly stopped and clutched my arm saying hardly above his breath:

"God! God! what is that?"

"I hear nothing," I replied.

"But see—see!" he said, pointing along the road directly ahead.

I said: "Nothing is there. Come, father, let us go in— you are ill."

He had released my arm and was standing rigid and motionless in the center of the illuminated roadway, staring like one bereft of sense. His face in the moonlight showed a pallor and fixity inexpressibly distressing. I pulled gently at his sleeve, but he had forgotten my existence. Presently he began to retire backward, step by step, never for an instant removing his eyes from what he saw, or thought he saw. I turned half round to follow, but stood irresolute. I do not recall any feeling of fear, unless a sudden chill was its physical manifestation. It seemed as if an icy wind had touched my face and enfolded my body from head to foot; I could feel the stir of it in my hair.

At that moment my attention was drawn to a light that suddenly streamed from an upper window of the house: one of the servants, awakened by what mysterious premonition of evil who can say and in obedience to an impulse that she was never able to name, had lit a lamp. When I turned to look for my father he was gone, and in all the years that have passed no whisper of his fate has come across the borderland of conjecture from the realm of the unknown.

❧

2: STATEMENT OF CASPAR GRATTAN

Today I am said to live; tomorrow, here in this room, will lie a senseless shape of clay that all too long was I. If anyone lift the cloth from the face of that unpleasant thing it will be in gratification of a mere morbid curiosity. Some, doubtless, will go further and inquire, "Who was he?" In this writing I supply the only answer that I am able to make—Caspar Grattan. Surely, that should be enough. The name has served my small need for more than 20 years of a life of unknown length. True, I gave it to myself, but lacking another I had the right. In this world one must have a name; it prevents confusion, even when it does not establish identity. Some, though, are known by numbers which also seem inadequate distinctions.

One day, for illustration, I was passing along a street of a city far from here, when I met two men in uniform, one of whom, half pausing and looking curiously into my face, said to his companion, "That man looks like 767." Something in the number seemed familiar and horrible. Moved by an uncontrollable impulse, I sprang into a side street and ran until I fell exhausted in a country lane.

I have never forgotten that number, and always it comes to memory attended by gibbering obscenity, peals of joyless laughter, the clang of iron doors. So I say a name, even if self-bestowed, is better than a number. In the register of the potter's field I shall soon have both. What wealth!

Of him who shall find this paper I must beg a little consideration. It is not the history of my life; the knowledge to write that is denied me. This is only a record of broken and apparently unrelated memories, some of them as distinct and sequent as brilliant beads upon a thread, others remote and strange having the character of crimson dreams with interspaces blank and black—witch fires glowing still and red in a great desolation.

Standing upon the shore of eternity, I turn for a last look landward over the course by which I came. There are 20 years of footprints fairly distinct, the impressions of bleeding feet. They lead through poverty and pain, devious and unsure, as of one staggering beneath a burden—

Remote, unfriended, melancholy, slow.

Ah, the poet's prophecy of me—how admirable, how dreadfully admirable!

Backward beyond the beginning of this via dolorosa—this epic of suffering with episodes of sin—I see nothing clearly; it comes out of a cloud. I know that it spans only 20 years, yet I am an old man.

One does not remember one's birth—one has to be told. But with me it was different; life came to me full-handed and dowered me with all my faculties and powers. Of a previous existence I know no more than others, for all have stammering intimations that may be memories and may be dreams. I know only that my first consciousness was of maturity in body and mind—a consciousness accepted without surprise or conjecture. I merely found myself walking in a forest, half-clad, footsore, unutterably weary and hungry. Seeing a farmhouse, I approached and asked for food which was given me by one who inquired my name. I did not know, yet knew that all had names. Greatly embarrassed, I retreated and night coming on lay down in the forest and slept.

The next day I entered a large town which I shall not name. Nor shall I recount further incidents of the life that is now to end—a life of wandering, always and everywhere haunted by an overmastering sense of crime in punishment of wrong and of terror in punishment of crime. Let me see if I can reduce it to narrative.

I seem once to have lived near a great city, a prosperous planter, married to a woman whom I loved and distrusted. We had, it sometimes seems, one child, a youth of brilliant parts and promise. He is at all times a vague figure, never clearly drawn, frequently altogether out of the picture.

One luckless evening it occurred to me to test my wife's fidelity in a vulgar, commonplace way familiar to everyone who has acquaintance with the literature of fact and fiction. I went to the city, telling my wife that I should be absent until the following afternoon. But I returned before daybreak and went to the rear of the house, purposing to enter by a door with which I had secretly so tampered that it would seem to lock, yet not actually fasten. As I approached it, I heard it gently open and close, and saw a man steal away into the darkness. With murder in my heart, I sprang after him, but he had vanished without even the bad luck of identification. Sometimes now I cannot even persuade myself that it was a human being.

Crazed with jealousy and rage, blind and bestial with all the elemental passions of insulted manhood, I entered the house and sprang up the stairs to the door of my wife's chamber. It was closed, but having tampered with its lock also, I easily entered and despite the black darkness soon stood by the side of her bed. My groping hands told me that although disarranged it was unoccupied.

"She is below," I thought, "and terrified by my entrance has evaded me in the darkness of the hall." With the purpose of seeking her I turned to leave the room, but took a wrong direction—the right one! My foot struck her cowering in a corner of the room. Instantly my hands were at her throat stifling a shriek, my knees were upon her struggling body; and there in the darkness without a word of accusation or reproach, I strangled her till she died! There ends the dream. I have related it in the past tense, but the present would be the fitter form, for again and again the somber tragedy re-enacts itself in my consciousness—over and over I lay the plan, I suffer the confirmation, I redress the wrong. Then all is blank; and afterward the rains beat against the grimy windowpanes, or the snows fall upon my scant attire. The wheels rattle in the squalid streets where my life lies in poverty and mean employment. If there is ever sunshine I do not recall it; if there are birds they do not sing.

There is another dream, another vision of the night. I stand among the shadows in a moonlit road. I am aware of another presence, but whose I cannot rightly determine. In the shadow of a great dwelling I catch the gleam of white garments; then the figure of a woman confronts me in the road—my murdered wife! There is death in the face; there are marks upon the throat. The eyes are fixed on mine with an infinite gravity which is not reproach, nor hate, nor menace, nor anything less terrible than recognition. Before this awful apparition I retreat in terror—a terror that is upon me as I write. I can no longer rightly shape the words. See! they—

Now I am calm, but truly there is no more to tell: the incident ends where it began—in darkness and in doubt.

Yes, I am again in control of myself: "the captain of my soul." But that is not respite; it is another stage and phase of expiation. My penance, constant in degree, is mutable in kind: one of its variants is tranquility. After all, it is only a life sentence. To hell for life—that is a foolish penalty: the culprit chooses the duration of his punishment. Today my term expires.

To each and all, the peace that was not mine.

※

3: STATEMENT OF THE LATE JULIA HETMAN, THROUGH THE MEDIUM BAYROLLES

I had retired early and fallen almost immediately into a peaceful sleep from which I awoke with that indefinable sense of peril which is, I think, a common experience in that other, earlier life. Of its unmeaning character, too, I was entirely persuaded, yet that did not banish it. My husband, Joel Hetman, was away from home; the servants slept in another part of the house. But these were familiar conditions; they

31

had never before distressed me. Nevertheless, the strange terror grew so insupportable that conquering my reluctance to move I sat up and lit the lamp at my bedside.

Contrary to my expectation this gave me no relief; the light seemed rather an added danger, for I reflected that it would shine out under the door, disclosing my presence to whatever evil thing might lurk outside. You that are still in the flesh, subject to horrors of the imagination, think what a monstrous fear that must be which seeks in darkness security from malevolent existences of the night. That is to spring to close quarters with an unseen enemy—the strategy of despair!

Extinguishing the lamp, I pulled the bedclothing about my head and lay trembling and silent, unable to shriek, forgetful to pray. In this pitiable state I must have lain for what you call hours—with us there are no hours, there is no time.

At last it came—a soft, irregular sound of footfalls on the stairs! They were slow, hesitant, uncertain, as of something that did not see its way; to my disordered reason all the more terrifying for that, as the approach of some blind and mindless malevolence to which is no appeal. I even thought that I must have left the hall lamp burning and the groping of this creature proved it a monster of the night. This was foolish and inconsistent with my previous dread of the light, but what would you have? Fear has no brains; it is an idiot. The dismal witness that it bears and the cowardly counsel that it whispers are unrelated. We know this well, we who have passed into the realm of terror, who skulk in eternal dusk among the scenes of our former lives, invisible even to ourselves and one another, yet hiding forlorn in lonely places; yearning for speech with our loved ones, yet dumb, and as fearful of them as they of us.

Sometimes the disability is removed, the law suspended by the deathless power of love or hate, we break the spell—we are seen by those whom we would warn, console, or punish. What form we seem to them to bear we know not; we know only that we terrify even those whom we most wish to comfort and from whom we most crave tenderness and sympathy.

Forgive, I pray you, this inconsequent digression by what was once a woman. You who consult us in this imperfect way—you do not understand. You ask foolish questions about things unknown and things forbidden. Much that we know and could impart in our speech is meaningless in yours. We must communicate with you through a stammering intelligence in that small fraction of our language that you yourselves can speak. You think that we are of another world. No, we have knowledge of no world but yours, though for us it holds no sunlight, no warmth, no music, no laughter, no song of birds, nor any companionship. O God! what a thing it is to be a ghost, cowering and shivering in an altered world, a prey to apprehension and despair!

No, I did not die of fright: the thing turned and went away. I heard it go down the stairs hurriedly, I thought, as if itself in sudden fear. Then I rose to call for help. Hardly had my shaking hand found the doorknob when—merciful heaven!—I heard it returning. Its footfalls as it remounted the stairs were rapid, heavy and loud; they shook the house. I fled to an angle of the wall and crouched upon the floor. I tried to pray. I tried to call the name of my dear husband. Then I heard the door thrown open. There was an interval of unconsciousness, and when I revived I felt a strangling clutch upon my throat—felt my arms feebly beating against something that bore me backward—felt my tongue thrusting itself from between my teeth! And then I passed into this life.

No, I have no knowledge of what it was. The sum of what we knew at death is the measure of what we know afterward of all that went before. Of this existence we know many things, but no new light falls upon any page of that; in memory is written all of it that we can read. Here are no heights of truth overlooking the confused landscape of that dubitable domain. We still dwell in the Valley of the Shadow, lurk in its desolate places, peering from brambles and thickets at its mad, malign inhabitants. How should we have new knowledge of that fading past?

What I am about to relate happened on a night. We know when it is night, for then you retire to your houses and we can venture from our places of concealment to move unafraid about our old homes, to look in at the windows, even to enter and gaze upon your faces as you sleep. I had lingered long near the dwelling where I had been so cruelly changed to what I am, as we do while any that we love or hate remain. Vainly I had sought some method of manifestation, some way to make my continued existence and my great love and poignant pity understood by my husband and son. Always if they slept they would wake, or if in my desperation I dared approach them when they were awake, would turn toward me the terrible eyes of the living, frightening me by the glances that I sought from the purpose that I held.

On this night I had searched for them without success, fearing to find them; they were nowhere in the house, nor about the moonlit dawn. For, although the sun is lost to us for ever, the moon, full orbed or slender, remains to us. Sometimes it shines by night, sometimes by day, but always it rises and sets, as in that other life.

I left the lawn and moved in the white light and silence along the road, aimless and sorrowing. Suddenly I heard the voice of my poor husband in exclamations of astonishment with that of my son in reassurance and dissuasion; and there by the shadow of a group of trees they stood—near, so near! Their faces were toward me, the eyes of the elder man fixed upon mine. He saw me—at last, at last, he saw me! In the consciousness of that, my terror fled as a cruel dream. The death spell was broken: love had conquered law! Mad with exultation I shouted—I must have shouted, "He sees, he sees: he will understand!" Then, controlling myself, I moved forward, smiling and consciously beautiful to offer myself to his arms, to comfort him with endearments, and, with my son's hand in mine, to speak words that should restore the broken bonds between the living and the dead.

Alas! alas! his face went white with fear, his eyes were as those of a hunted animal. He backed away from me as I advanced, and at last turned and fled into the wood—whither, it is not given to me to know.

To my poor boy, left doubly desolate, I have never been able to impart a sense of my presence. Soon he, too, must pass to this life invisible and be lost to me for ever.

THE SCREAMING SKULL (1911)

by

F. Marion Crawford

(1854–1909)

Francis Marion Crawford, *an American, was a master of many languages: English, of course, the European languages, as well as Turkish, Russian, a number of Eastern languages, and Sanskrit. And yet, great intellect that he was (he wrote more than 40 novels in 25 years), he believed that writing should be only for entertainment. He called novels "pocket theaters." His books were light and adventurous. Some had historical settings. A few were tales of horror; and a number of others, it is for these that Crawford is best remembered.*

"The Screaming Skull" begins much like Edgar Allan Poe's famous story "The Tell-tale Heart." The narrator declares at length how calm and rational he is. But unlike Poe, Crawford invites you, the reader, directly into the tale. You are one of the characters. The writing is vivid. It takes little imagination to enter the story and set yourself down in a comfortable chair and listen, but the old man's rambling begins to get on your nerves. You're ready to turn to a different story when you hear it, too . . . There it is again—that horrifying scream!

I HAVE OFTEN HEARD IT SCREAM. NO, I AM NOT NERVOUS, I am not imaginative, and I never believed in ghosts, unless that thing is one. Whatever it is, it hates me almost as much as it hated Luke Pratt, and it screams at me.

If I were you, I would never tell ugly stories about ingenious ways of killing people, for you never can tell but that someone at the table may be tired of his or her nearest and dearest. I have always blamed myself for Mrs. Pratt's death, and I suppose I was responsible for it in a way, though heaven knows I never wished her anything but long life and happiness. If I had not told that story, she might be alive yet. That is why the thing screams at me, I fancy.

She was a good little woman with a sweet temper, all things considered, and a nice gentle voice; but I remember hearing her shriek once when she thought her little boy was killed by a pistol that went off though everyone was sure that it was not loaded. It was the same scream; exactly the same with a sort of rising quaver at the end. Do you know what I mean? Unmistakable.

The truth is, I had not realized that the doctor and his wife were not on good terms. They used to bicker a bit now and then when I was here, and I often noticed that little Mrs. Pratt got very red and bit her lip hard to keep her temper, while Luke grew pale and said the most offensive things. He was that sort when he was in the nursery, I remember, and afterward at school. He was my cousin, you know; that is how I came by this house. After he died and his boy Charley was killed in South Africa, there were no relations left. Yes, it's a pretty little property. Just the sort of thing for an old sailor like me who has taken to gardening.

One always remembers one's mistakes much more vividly than one's cleverest things, doesn't one? I've often noticed it. I was dining with the Pratts one night, when I told them the story that afterward made so much difference. It was a wet night in November, and the sea was moaning. Hush!—if you don't speak you will hear it now . . .

Do you hear the tide? Gloomy sound, isn't it? Sometimes, about this time of year—hallo!—there it is! Don't be frightened, man—it won't eat you—it's only a noise, after all! But I'm glad you've heard it, because there are always people who think it's the wind, or my imagination, or something. You won't hear it again tonight, I fancy, for it doesn't often come more than once.

Yes—that's right. Put another stick on the fire, and a little more stuff into that weak mixture you're so fond of.

The weather was dirty, Pratt was out of temper, and the dinner was bad, very bad indeed, which didn't improve matters, and cold, which made it worse. The poor little lady was very unhappy about it and insisted on making a Welsh rarebit on the table to counteract the raw turnips and the half-boiled mutton. Pratt must have had a hard day. Perhaps he had lost a patient. At all events, he was in a nasty temper.

"My wife is trying to poison me, you see!" he said. "She'll succeed some day." I saw that she was hurt, and I made believe to laugh and said that Mrs. Pratt was much too clever to get rid of her husband in such a simple way. Then I began to tell them about Japanese tricks with spun glass and chopped horsehair and the like.

Pratt was a doctor and knew a lot more than I did about such things, but that only put me on my mettle, and I told a story about a woman in Ireland who did for three husbands before anyone suspected foul play.

Did you never hear that tale? The fourth husband managed to keep awake and caught her, and she was hanged. How did she do it? She drugged them, and poured melted lead into their ears through a little horn funnel when they were asleep . . . No—that's the wind whistling. It's backing up to the southward again. I can tell by the sound. Besides, the other thing doesn't often come more than once in an evening even at this time of year—when it happened. Yes, it was in November. Poor Mrs. Pratt died suddenly in her bed not long after I dined here. I can fix the date, because I got the news in New York by the steamer that followed the *Olympia* when I took her out on her first trip. You had the *Leofric* the same year? Yes, I remember. What a pair of old buffers we are coming to be, you and I. Nearly fifty years since we were apprentices together on the *Clontarf*.

Where did I leave off? I told you that Mrs. Pratt died suddenly—yes. Luke must have been lonely here after she was dead, I should think. I came to see him now and then, and he looked worn and nervous and told me that his practice was growing too heavy for him though he wouldn't take an assistant on any account. Years went on, and his son was killed in South Africa, and after that he began to be odd. There was something about him not like other people. I believe he kept his senses in his profession to the end. There was no complaint of his having made mad mistakes in cases, or anything of that sort, but he had a look about him.

Luke was a red-headed man with a pale face when he was young, and he was never stout; in middle age he turned a sandy gray, and after his son died he grew thinner and thinner till his head looked like a skull with parchment stretched over it very tight. His eyes had a sort of glare in them that was very disagreeable to look at.

He had an old dog that poor Mrs. Pratt had been fond of and that used to follow her everywhere. He was a bulldog, and the sweetest tempered beast you ever saw though he had a way of hitching his upper lip behind one of his fangs that frightened strangers a good deal.

Sometimes, of an evening, Pratt and Bumble—that was the dog's name—used to sit and look at each other a long time thinking about old times, I suppose, when Luke's wife used to sit in that chair you've got. That was always her place, and this was the doctor's where I'm sitting. Bumble used to climb up by the footstool—he was old and fat by that time and could not jump much, and his teeth were getting shaky. He would look steadily at Luke, and Luke looked steadily at the dog, his face growing more and more like a skull with two little coals for eyes. After about five minutes or so, though it may have been less, old Bumble would suddenly begin to shake all over, and all of a sudden he would set up an awful howl as if he had been shot and tumble out of the easy chair and trot away and hide himself under the sideboard and lie there making odd noises.

Considering Pratt's looks in those last months, the thing is not surprising, you know. I'm not nervous or imaginative, but I can quite believe he might have sent a sensitive woman into hysterics—his head looked so much like a skull in parchment.

At last I came down one day before Christmas, when my ship was in dock and I had three weeks off. Bumble was not about, and I said casually that I supposed the old dog was dead.

"Yes," Pratt answered, and I thought there was something odd in his tone even before he went on after a little pause. "I killed him," he said presently. "I could stand it no longer."

I asked what it was that Luke could not stand, though I guessed well enough.

"He had a way of sitting in her chair and glaring at me and then howling," Luke shivered a little. "He didn't suffer at all, poor old Bumble," he went on in a hurry, as if he thought I might imagine he had been cruel. "I put dionine into his drink to make him sleep soundly, and then I chloroformed him gradually so that he could not have felt suffocated even if he was dreaming. It's been quieter since then."

I wondered what he meant for the words slipped out as if he could not help saying them. I've understood since. He meant that he did not hear that noise so often after the dog was out of the way. Perhaps he thought at first that it was old Bumble in the yard howling at the moon, though it's not that kind of noise, is it?

Besides, I know what it is, if Luke didn't. It's only a noise after all, and a noise never hurt anybody yet. But he was much more imaginative than I am. No doubt there really is something about this place that I don't understand; but when I don't understand a thing, I call it a phenomenon, and I don't take it for granted that it's going to kill me, as he did.

Besides, what is there to prove that Luke killed his wife? I would not even suggest such a thing to anyone but you. After all, there was nothing but the coincidence that poor little Mrs. Pratt died suddenly in her bed a few days after I told that story at dinner. She was not the only woman who ever died like that. Luke got the doctor over from the next parish, and they agreed that she had died of something the matter with her heart. Why not? It's common enough.

Of course, there was the ladle. I never told anybody about that, and, it made me start when I found it in the cupboard in the bedroom. It was new, too—a little tinned iron ladle that had not been in the fire more than once or twice, and there was some lead in it that had been melted and stuck to the bottom of the bowl, all gray, with hardened dross on it.

But that proves nothing. A country doctor is generally a handy man, who does everything for himself, and Luke may have had a dozen reasons for melting a little lead in a ladle. He was fond of sea fishing, for instance, and he may have cast a sinker for a night line. Perhaps it was a weight for the hall clock or something like that. All the same, when I found it I had a rather odd sensation, because it looked so much like the thing I had described when I told them the story. Do you understand? It affected me unpleasantly, and I threw it away; it's at the bottom of the sea a mile from the Spit, and it will be jolly well rusted beyond recognizing if it's ever washed up by the tide.

You see, Luke must have bought it in the village, years ago, for the man sells just such ladles still. I suppose they are used in cooking. In any case, there was no reason why an inquisitive housemaid should find such a thing lying about with lead in it and wonder what it was and perhaps talk to the maid who heard me tell the story at dinner—for that girl married the plumber's son in the village and may remember the whole thing.

You understand me, don't you? Now that Luke Pratt is dead and gone and lies buried beside his wife with an honest man's tombstone at his head, I should not care to stir up anything that could hurt his memory. They are both dead and their son, too. There was trouble enough about Luke's death as it was.

How? He was found dead on the beach one morning, and there was a coroner's inquest. There were marks on his throat, but he had not been robbed. The verdict was that he had come to his end "By the hands or teeth of some person or animal unknown," for half the jury thought it might have been a big dog that had thrown him down and gripped his windpipe, though the skin of his throat was not broken. No one knew at what time he had gone out, nor where he had been. He was found lying on his back above high-water mark and an old cardboard bandbox that had belonged to his wife lay under his hand open. The lid had fallen off. He seemed to have been carrying home a skull in the box—doctors are fond of collecting such things. It had rolled out and lay near his head, and it was a remarkably fine skull, rather small, beautifully shaped and very white with perfect teeth. That is to say, the upper jaw was perfect, but there was no lower one at all when I first saw it.

Yes, I found it here when I came. You see, it was very white and polished like a thing meant to be kept under a glass case. The people did not know where it came from, nor what to do with it; so they put it back into the bandbox and set it on the shelf of the cupboard in the best bedroom, and of course they showed it to me when I took possession. I was taken down to the beach, too, to be shown the place where Luke was found, and the old fisherman explained just how he was lying and the skull beside him.

The only point he could not explain was why the skull had rolled up the sloping sand toward Luke's head instead of rolling downhill to his feet. It did not seem odd to me at the time, but I have often thought of it since, for the place is rather steep. I'll take you there tomorrow if you like—I made a sort of cairn of stones there afterward.

When he fell down or was thrown down—whichever happened—the bandbox struck the sand, and the lid came off, and the thing came out and ought to have rolled down. But it didn't. It was close to his head almost touching it and turned with the face toward it. I say it didn't strike me as odd when the man told me; but I could not help thinking about it afterward, again and again, till I saw a picture of it all when I closed my eyes; and then I began to ask myself why the plaguey thing had rolled up instead of down, and why it had stopped near Luke's head instead of anywhere else, a yard away, for instance.

You naturally want to know what conclusion I reached, don't you? None that at all explained the rolling, at all events. But I got something else into my head, after a time, that made me feel downright uncomfortable.

Oh, I don't mean as to anything supernatural! There may be ghosts, or there may not be. If there are, I'm not inclined to believe that they can hurt living people except by frightening them, and for my part I would rather face any shape of ghost than a fog in the Channel when it's crowded. No. What bothered me was just a foolish idea, that's all, and I cannot tell how it began, nor what made it grow till it turned into a certainty.

I was thinking about Luke and his poor wife one evening over my pipe and a dull book when it occurred to me that the skull might possibly be hers, and I have never got rid of the thought since. You'll tell me there's no sense in it, no doubt, that Mrs. Pratt was buried like a Christian and is lying in the churchyard where they put her, and that it's perfectly monstrous to suppose her husband kept her skull in her old bandbox in his bedroom.

All the same, in the face of reason and common sense and probability, I'm convinced that he did. Doctors do all sorts of strange things that would make men like you and me feel creepy, and those are just the things that don't seem probable, nor logical, nor sensible to us.

Then, don't you see?—if it really was her skull, poor woman, the only way of accounting for his having it is that he really killed her and did it in that way as the woman killed her husbands in the story, and that he was afraid there might be an examination some day which would betray him. You see, I told that too, and I believe it had really happened some fifty or sixty years ago. They dug up the three skulls, you know, and there was a small lump of lead rattling about in each one. That was what hanged the woman. Luke remembered that, I'm sure. I don't want to know what he did when he thought of it; my taste never ran in the direction of horrors, and I don't fancy you care for them either, do you? No. If you did, you might supply what is wanting to the story.

It must have been rather grim, eh? I wish I did not see the whole thing so distinctly just as everything must have happened. He took it the night before she was buried, I'm sure, after the coffin had been shut and when the servant girl was asleep. I would bet anything that when he'd got it, he put something under the sheet in its place to fill up and look like it. What do you suppose he put there under the sheet?

I don't wonder you take me up on what I'm saying! First I tell you that I don't want to know what happened, and that I hate to think about horrors, and then I describe the whole thing to you as if I had seen it. I'm quite sure that it was her workbag that he put there. I remember the bag very well, for she always used it of an evening; it was made of brown plush, and when it was stuffed full it was about the size of—you understand.

Yes, there I am at it again! You may laugh at me, but you don't live here alone where it was done, and you didn't tell Luke the story about the melted lead. I'm not nervous, I tell you, but sometimes I begin to feel that I understand why some people are. I dwell on all this when I'm alone, and I dream of it, and when that thing screams—well, frankly, I don't like the noise any more than you do, though I should be used to it by this time.

I ought not to be nervous. I've sailed in a haunted ship. There was a Man in the Top, and two-thirds of the crew died of the West Coast fever inside of 10 days after we anchored; but I was all right, then and afterward. I have seen some ugly sights, too, just as you have and all the rest of us. But nothing ever stuck in my head in the way this does.

You see, I've tried to get rid of the thing, but it doesn't like that. It wants to be there in its place, in Mrs. Pratt's bandbox in the cupboard in the best bedroom. It's not happy anywhere else. How do I know that? Because I've tried it. You don't suppose that I've not tried, do you? As long as it's there it only screams now and then, generally at this time

45

of year, but if I put it out of the house it goes on all night, and no servant will stay here 24 hours.

As it is, I've often been left alone and have been obliged to shift for myself for two weeks at a time. No one from the village would ever pass a night under the roof now, and as for selling the place or even letting it, that's out of the question. The old women say that if I stay here I shall come to a bad end myself before long.

I'm not afraid of that. You smile at the mere idea that anyone could take such nonsense seriously. Quite right. It's utterly blatant nonsense, I agree with you. Didn't I tell you that it's only a noise after all when you started and looked round as if you expected to see a ghost standing behind your chair?

I may be all wrong about the skull, and I like to think that I am when I can. It may be just a fine specimen which Luke got somewhere long ago, and what rattles about inside when you shake it may be nothing but a pebble or a bit of hard clay or anything. Skulls that have lain long in the ground generally have something inside them that rattles don't they?

No, I've never tried to get it out, whatever it is. I'm afraid it might be lead, don't you see? And if it is, I don't want to know the fact, for I'd much rather not be sure. If it really is lead, I killed her quite as much as if I had done the deed myself. Anybody must see that, I should think. As long as I don't know for certain, I have the consolation of saying that it's all utterly ridiculous nonsense, that Mrs. Pratt died a natural death and that the beautiful skull belonged to Luke when he was a student in London. But if I were quite sure, I believe I should have to leave the house; indeed I do, most certainly. As it is, I had to give up trying to sleep in the best bedroom where the cupboard is.

You ask me why I don't throw it into the pond—yes, but please don't call it a "confounded bugbear"—it doesn't like being called names.

There! Lord, what a shriek! I told you so! You're quite pale, man. Fill up your pipe and draw your chair nearer to the fire, and take some more drink. Old Hollands never hurt anybody yet. I've seen a Dutchman in Java drink half a jug of Hulstkamp in a morning without turning a hair. I don't take much rum myself, because it doesn't agree with my rheumatism, but you are not rheumatic and it won't damage you. Besides, it's a very damp night outside. The wind is howling again, and it will soon be in the south-west; do you hear how the windows rattle? The tide must have turned too, by the moaning.

We should not have heard the thing again if you had not said that. I'm pretty sure we should not. Oh yes, if you choose to describe it as a coincidence, you are quite welcome, but I would rather that you should not call the thing names again, if you don't mind. It may be that the poor little woman hears, and perhaps it hurts her, don't you know? Ghosts? No! You don't call anything a ghost that you can take in your hands and look at in broad daylight and that rattles when you shake it. Do you, now? But it's something that hears and understands; there's no doubt about that.

I tried sleeping in the best bedroom when I first came to the house just because it was the best and most comfortable, but I had to give it up. It was their room, and there's the big bed she died in, and the cupboard is in the thickness of the wall near the head on the left. That's where it likes to be kept, in its bandbox. I only used the room for two weeks after I came, and then I turned out and took the little room downstairs next to the surgery where Luke used to sleep when he expected to be called to a patient during the night.

I was always a good sleeper ashore; eight hours is my dose, eleven to seven when I'm alone, twelve to eight when I have a friend with me. But I could not sleep after three o'clock in the morning in that room—a quarter past, to be accurate—as a matter of fact, I timed it with my old pocket chronometer which still keeps good time, and it was always at exactly seventeen minutes past three. I wonder whether that was the hour when she died?

It was not what you have heard. If it had been that, I could not have stood it two nights. It was just a start and a moan and hard breathing for a few seconds in the cupboard, and it could never have waked me under ordinary circumstances, I'm sure. I suppose you are like me in that, and we are just like other people who have been to sea. No natural sounds disturb us at all, not all the racket of a square-rigger hove to in a heavy gale or rolling on her beam ends before the wind. But if a lead pencil gets adrift and rattles in the drawer of your cabin table you are awake in a moment. Just so—you always understand. Very well, the noise in the cupboard was no louder than that, but it waked me instantly.

I said it was like a start. I know what I mean, but it's hard to explain without seeming to talk nonsense. Of course you cannot exactly hear a person start; at the most you might hear the quick drawing of the breath between the parted lips and closed teeth and the almost imperceptible sound of clothing that moved suddenly though very slightly. It was like that.

You know how one feels what a sailing vessel is going to do, two or three seconds before she does it when one has the wheel. Riders say the same of a horse, but that's less strange because the horse is a live animal with feelings of its own, and only poets and landsmen talk about a ship being alive and all that. But I have always felt somehow that besides

48

being a steaming machine or a sailing machine for carrying weights, a vessel at sea is a sensitive instrument and a means of communication between nature and man and most particularly the man at the wheel if she is steered by hand. She takes her impressions directly from wind and sea, tide and stream and transmits them to the man's hand just as the wireless telegraph picks up the interrupted currents aloft and turns them out below in the form of a message.

You see what I am driving at; I felt that something started in the cupboard, and I felt it so vividly that I heard it though there may have been nothing to hear, and the sound inside my head waked me suddenly. But I really heard the other noise. It was as if it were muffled inside a box as far away as if it came through a long-distance telephone; and yet I knew that it was inside the cupboard near the head of my bed. My hair did not bristle and my blood did not run cold that time. I simply resented being waked up by something that had no business to make a noise any more than a pencil should rattle in the drawer of my cabin table on board ship. For I did not understand; I just supposed that the cupboard had some communication with the outside air, and that the wind had got in and was moaning through it with a sort of very faint screech.

I struck a light and looked at my watch, and it was seventeen minutes past three. Then I turned over and went to sleep on my right ear. That's my good one; I'm pretty deaf with the other, for I struck the water with it when I was a lad in diving from the fore-topsail yard. Silly thing to do, it was, but the result is very convenient when I want to go to sleep when there's a noise.

That was the first night, and the same thing happened again and several times afterward, but not regularly though it was always at the same time to a second; perhaps I was sometimes sleeping on my good ear and sometimes not. I overhauled the cupboard, and there was no way by which the wind could get in or anything else, for the door makes a good fit, having been meant to keep out moths, I suppose; Mrs. Pratt must have kept her winter things in it, for it still smells of camphor and turpentine.

After about two weeks I had had enough of the noises. So far I had said to myself that it would be silly to yield to it and take the skull out of the room. Things always look differently by daylight, don't they? But the voice grew louder—I suppose one may call it a voice—and it got inside my deaf ear, too, one night. I realized that when I was wide awake, for my good ear was jammed down on the pillow, and I ought not to have heard a foghorn in that position. But I heard that, and it made me lose my temper, unless it scared me, for sometimes the two are not far apart. I struck a light and got up, and I opened the cupboard, grabbed the bandbox and threw it out of the window as far as I could.

Then my hair stood on end. The thing screamed in the air like a shell from a 12-inch gun. It fell on the other side of the road. The night was very dark, and I could not see it fall, but I know it fell beyond the road. The window is just over the front door; it's 15 yards to the fence, more or less, and the road is 10 yards wide. There's a thickset hedge beyond that belongs to the vicarage.

I did not sleep much more that night. It was not more than half an hour after I had thrown the bandbox out when I heard a shriek outside—like what we've had tonight, but worse, more despairing, I should call it; and it may have been my imagination, but I could have sworn that the screams came nearer and nearer each time. I lit a pipe and walked up and down for a bit and then took a book and sat up reading, but I'll be hanged if I can remember what I read nor even what the book was, for every now and then a shriek came up that would have made a dead man turn in his coffin.

A little before dawn someone knocked at the front door. There was no mistaking that for anything else, and I opened my window and looked down, for I guessed that someone wanted the doctor, supposing that the new man had taken Luke's house. It was rather a relief to hear a human knock after that awful noise.

You cannot see the door from above, owing to the little porch. The knocking came again, and I called out asking who was there, but nobody answered, though the knock was repeated. I sang out again and said that the doctor did not live here any longer. There was no answer, but it occurred to me that it might be some old countryman who was stone deaf. So I took my candle and went down to open the door. Upon my word, I was not thinking of the thing yet, and I had almost forgotten the other noises. I went down convinced that I should find somebody outside, on the doorstep, with a message. I set the candle on the hall table, so that the wind should not blow it out when I opened. While I was drawing the old-fashioned bolt I heard the knocking again. It was not loud, and it had an odd, hollow sound now that I was close to it, I remember, but I certainly thought it was made by some person who wanted to get in.

It wasn't. There was nobody there, but as I opened the door inward standing a little on one side so as to see out, at once something rolled across the threshold and stopped against my foot.

I drew back as I felt it, for I knew what it was before I looked down. I cannot tell you how I knew, and it seemed unreasonable, for I am still quite sure that I had thrown it across the road. It's a French window that opens wide, and I got a good swing when I flung it out. Besides, when I went out early in the morning, I found the bandbox beyond the thick hedge.

You may think it opened when I threw it, and that the skull dropped out; but that's impossible, for nobody could throw an empty cardboard box so far. It's out of the question; you might as well try to fling a ball of paper 25 yards or a blown bird's egg.

To go back, I shut and bolted the hall door, picked the thing up carefully, and put it on the table beside the candle. I did that mechanically, as one instinctively does the right thing in danger without thinking at all—unless one does the opposite. It may seem odd, but I believe my first thought had been that somebody might come and find me there on the threshold while it was resting against my foot, lying a little on its side and turning one hollow eye up at my face as if it meant to accuse me. And the light and shadow from the candle played in the hollows of the eyes as it stood on the table so that they seemed to open and shut at me.

Then the candle went out quite unexpectedly, though the door was fastened and there was not the least draught; and I used up at least half a dozen matches before it would burn again.

I sat down rather suddenly without quite knowing why. Probably I had been badly frightened, and perhaps you will admit there was no great shame in being scared. The thing had come home, and it wanted to go upstairs back to its cupboard. I sat still and stared at it for a bit till I began to feel very cold; then I took it and carried it up and set it in its place, and I remember that I spoke to it and promised that it should have its bandbox again in the morning.

You want to know whether I stayed in the room till daybreak? Yes, but I kept a light burning and sat up smoking and reading, most likely out of fright; plain, undeniable fear,

and you need not call it cowardice either, for that's not the same thing. I could not have stayed alone with that thing in the cupboard; I should have been scared to death though I'm not more timid than other people. Confound it all, man, it had crossed the road alone and had got up the doorstep and had knocked to be let in.

When the dawn came, I put on my boots and went out to find the bandbox. I had to go a good way round by the gate near the high road, and I found the box open and hanging on the other side of the hedge. It had caught on the twigs by the string, and the lid had fallen off and was lying on the ground below it. That shows that it did not open till it was well over; and if it had not opened as soon as it left my hand, what was inside it must have gone beyond the road too.

That's all. I took the box upstairs to the cupboard and put the skull back and locked it up. When the girl brought me my breakfast, she said she was sorry, but that she must go, and she did not care if she lost her month's wages. I looked at her, and her face was a sort of greenish yellowish white. I pretended to be surprised and asked what was the matter; but that was of no use, for she just turned on me and wanted to know whether I meant to stay in a haunted house, and how long I expected to live if I did, for though she noticed I was sometimes a little hard of hearing, she did not believe that even I could sleep through those screams again—and if I could, why had I been moving about the house and opening and shutting the front door, between three and four in the morning?

There was no answering that since she had heard me, so off she went, and I was left to myself. I went down to the village during the morning and found a woman who was willing to come and do the little work there is and cook my dinner on condition that she might go home every night. As for me, I moved downstairs that day, and I have never tried to sleep in the best bedroom since. After a little while I got a couple of middle-aged Scotch servants from London, and things were quiet enough for a long time. I began by telling them that the house was in a very exposed position, and that the wind whistled round it a good deal in the autumn and winter, which had given it a bad name in the village, the Cornish people being inclined to superstition and telling ghost stories.

The two hard-faced, sandy-haired sisters almost smiled, and they answered with great contempt that they had no great opinion of any southern bogey whatever, having been in service in two English haunted houses where they had never seen so much as the Boy in Gray, whom they reckoned no very particular rarity in Forfarshire.

They stayed with me several months, and while they were in the house we had peace and quiet. One of them is here again now, but she went away with her sister within the year. This one—she was the cook—married the sexton, who works in my garden. That's the way of it. It's a small village and he has not much to do, and he knows enough about flowers to help me nicely, besides doing most of the hard work; for though I'm fond of exercise, I'm getting a little stiff in the hinges. He's a sober, silent sort of fellow who minds his own business, and he was a widower when I came here—Trehearn is his name, James Trehearn.

The Scottish sisters would not admit that there was anything wrong about the house, but when November came they gave me warning that they were going on the ground that the chapel was such a long walk from here, being in the next parish, and that they could not possibly go to our church. But the younger one came back in the spring, and as soon as the banns could be published she was married to

James Trehearn by the vicar, and she seems to have had no scruples about hearing him preach since then. I'm quite satisfied, if she is! The couple live in a small cottage that looks over the churchyard.

I suppose you are wondering what all this has to do with what I was talking about. I'm alone so much that when an old friend comes to see me, I sometimes go on talking just for the sake of hearing my own voice. But in this case there is really a connection of ideas. It was James Trehearn who buried poor Mrs. Pratt, and her husband after her in the same grave, and it's not far from the back of his cottage. That's the connection in my mind, you see. It's plain enough. He knows something; I'm quite sure that he does, though he's such a reticent beggar.

Yes, I'm alone in the house at night now, for Mrs. Trehearn does everything herself, and when I have a friend, the sexton's niece comes in to wait on the table. He takes his wife home every evening in winter, but in summer when there's light she goes by herself. She's not a nervous woman, but she's less sure than she used to be that there are no bogies in England worth a Scotch woman's notice. Isn't it amusing, the idea that Scotland has a monopoly of the supernatural? Odd sort of national pride, I call that, don't you?

That's a good fire, isn't it? When driftwood gets started at last there's nothing like it, I think. Yes, we get lots of it, for I'm sorry to say there are still a great many wrecks about here. It's a lonely coast, and you may have all the wood you want for the trouble of bringing it in. Trehearn and I borrow a cart now and then and load it between here and the Spit. I hate a coal fire when I can get wood of any sort. A log is company, even if it's only a piece of a deck beam or timber sawn off, and the salt in it makes pretty sparks. See how they fly, like Japanese hand fireworks! Upon my word, with an old friend and a good fire and a pipe, one forgets all about that thing upstairs, especially now that the wind has moderated. It's only a lull, though, and it will blow a gale before morning.

You think you would like to see the skull? I've no objection. There's no reason why you shouldn't have a look at it, and you never saw a more perfect one in your life, except that there are two front teeth missing in the lower jaw.

Oh yes—I had not told you about the jaw yet. Trehearn found it in the garden last spring when he was digging a pit for a new asparagus bed. You know we make asparagus beds six or eight feet deep here. Yes, yes—I had forgotten to tell you that. He was digging straight down, just as he digs a grave; if you want a good asparagus bed made, I advise you to get a sexton to make it for you. Those fellows have a wonderful knack at that sort of digging.

Trehearn had got down about three feet when he cut into a mass of white lime in the side of the trench. He had noticed that the earth was a little looser there, though he says it had not been disturbed for a number of years. I suppose he thought that even old lime might not be good for asparagus, so he broke it out and threw it up. It was pretty hard, he says, in biggish lumps, and out of sheer force of habit he cracked the lumps with his spade as they lay outside the pit beside him; the jawbone of the skull dropped out of one of the pieces.

He thinks he must have knocked out the two front teeth in breaking up the lime, but he did not see them anywhere. He's a very experienced man in such things, as you may imagine, and he said at once that the jaw had probably belonged to a young woman, and that the teeth had been complete when she died. He brought it to me and asked me if I wanted to keep it; if I did not, he said he would drop it into the next grave he made in the churchyard as he supposed it

57

was a Christian jaw and ought to have a decent burial, wherever the rest of the body might be. I told him that doctors often put bones into quicklime to whiten them nicely, and that I supposed Dr. Pratt had once had a little lime pit in the garden for that purpose and had forgotten the jaw. Trehearn looked at me quietly.

"Maybe it fitted that skull that used to be in the cupboard upstairs, sir," he said. "Maybe Dr. Pratt had put the skull into the lime to clean it or something, and when he took it out he left the lower jaw behind. There's some human hair sticking in the lime, sir."

I saw there was, and that was what Trehearn said. If he did not suspect something, why in the world should he have suggested that the jaw might fit the skull? Besides, it did. That's proof that he knows more than he cares to tell. Do you suppose he looked before she was buried? Or perhaps—when he buried Luke in the same grave.

Well, well, it's of no use to go over that, is it? I said I would keep the jaw with the skull, and I took it upstairs and fitted it into its place. There's not the slightest doubt about the two belonging together, and together they are.

Trehearn knows several things. We were talking about plastering the kitchen a while ago, and he happened to remember that it had not been done since the very week when Mrs. Pratt died. He did not say that the mason must have left some lime on the place, but he thought it, and that it was the very same lime he had found in the asparagus pit. He knows a lot. Trehearn is one of your silent beggars who can put two and two together. That grave is very near the back of his cottage, too, and he's one of the quickest men with a spade I ever saw. If he wanted to know the truth, he could, and no one else would ever be the wiser unless he chose to tell. In a quiet village like ours, people don't go and spend the night in the churchyard to see whether the sexton potters about by himself between ten o'clock and daylight.

What is awful to think of is Luke's deliberation, if he did it; his cool certainty that no one would find him out; above all, his nerve, for that must have been extraordinary. I sometimes think it's bad enough to live in the place where it was done, if it really was done. I always put in the condition, you see, for the sake of his memory, and a little bit for my own sake, too.

I'll go upstairs and fetch the box in a minute. Let me light my pipe; there's no hurry! We had supper early, and it's only half-past nine o'clock. I never let a friend go to bed before twelve or with less than three glasses—you may have as many more as you like, but you shan't have less, for the sake of old times.

It's breezing up again, do you hear? That was only a lull just now, and we are going to have a bad night.

A thing happened that made me start a little when I found that the jaw fitted exactly. I'm not very easily startled in that way myself, but I have seen people make a quick movement, drawing their breath sharply when they had thought they were alone and suddenly turned and saw someone very near them. Nobody can call that fear. You wouldn't, would you?

No. Well, just when I had set the jaw in its place under the skull, the teeth closed sharply on my finger. It felt exactly as if it were biting me hard, and I confess that I jumped before I realized that I had been pressing the jaw and the skull together with my other hand. I assure you I was not at all nervous. It was broad daylight, too, and a fine day, and the sun was streaming into the best bedroom. It would have been absurd to be nervous; and it was only a quick mistaken impression, but it really made me feel strange.

59

Somehow it made me think of the funny verdict of the coroner's jury on Luke's death: "by the hand or teeth of some person or animal unknown." Ever since that I've wished I had seen those marks on his throat, though the lower jaw was missing then.

I have often seen a man do insane things with his hands that he does not realize at all. I once saw a man hanging on by an old awning stop with one hand, leaning backward, outboard, with all his weight on it, and he was just cutting the stop with the knife in his other hand when I got my arms round him. We were in mid-ocean, going 20 knots. He had not the smallest idea what he was doing; neither had I when I managed to pinch my finger between the teeth of that thing. I can feel it now. It was exactly as if it were alive and were trying to bite me. It would if it could, for I know it hates me, poor thing!

Do you suppose that what rattles about inside is really a bit of lead? Well, I'll get the box down presently, and if whatever it is happens to drop out into your hands, that's your affair. If it's only a clod of earth or a pebble, the whole matter would be off my mind, and I don't believe I should ever think of the skull again; but somehow I cannot bring myself to shake out the bit of hard stuff myself. The mere idea that it may be lead makes me confoundedly uncomfortable, yet I've got the conviction that I shall know before long. I shall certainly know. I'm sure Trehearn knows, but he's such a silent beggar.

I'll go upstairs now and get it. What? You had better go with me? Ha, ha! do you think I'm afraid of a bandbox and a noise? Nonsense!

Bother the candle, it won't light! As if the ridiculous thing understood what it's wanted for! Look at that—the third match. They light fast enough for my pipe. There, do you see? It's a fresh box just out of the tin safe where I keep the supply on account of the dampness. Oh, you think the wick of the candle may be damp, do you? All right, I'll light the beastly thing in the fire. That won't go out, at all events. Yes, it sputters a bit, but it will keep lighted now. It burns just like any other candle, doesn't it? The fact is, candles are not very good about here. I don't know where they come from, but they have a way of burning low occasionally with a greenish flame that spits tiny sparks, and I'm often annoyed by their going out of themselves. It cannot be helped, for it will be long before we have electricity in our village. It really is rather a poor light, isn't it?

You think I had better leave you the candle and take the lamp, do you? I don't like to carry lamps about, that's the truth. I never dropped one in my life, but I have always thought I might, and it's so confoundedly dangerous if you do. Besides, I am pretty well used to these rotten candles by this time.

❧

Here's the box. I brought it down very carefully, so as not to disturb it, poor thing. You see, if it were shaken, the jaw might get separated from it again, and I'm sure it wouldn't like that. Yes, the candle went out as I was coming downstairs, but that was the draught from the leaky window on the landing. Did you hear anything? Yes, there was another scream. Am I pale, do you say? That's nothing. My heart is a little faint sometimes, and I went upstairs too fast. In fact, that's one reason why I really prefer to live altogether on the ground floor.

Wherever the shriek came from, it was not from the skull, for I had the box in my hand when I heard the noise, and here it is now; so we have proved definitely that the

61

screams are produced by something else. I've no doubt I shall find out some day what makes them. Some crevice in the wall, of course, or a crack in a chimney, or a chink in the frame of a window. That's the way all ghost stories end in real life. Do you know, I'm jolly glad I thought of going up and bringing it down for you to see, for that last shriek settles the question. To think that I should have been so weak as to fancy that the poor skull could really cry out like a living thing!

Now I'll open the box, and we'll take it out and look at it under the bright light. It's rather awful to think that the poor lady used to sit there, in your chair, evening after evening, in just the same light, isn't it? But then—I've made up my mind that it's all rubbish from beginning to end, and that it's just an old skull that Luke had when he was a student and perhaps he put it into the lime merely to whiten it and could not find the jaw.

I made a seal on the string, you see, after I had put the jaw in its place, and I wrote on the cover. There's the old white label on it still from the milliner's addressed to Mrs. Pratt when the hat was sent to her, and as there was room I wrote on the edge: "A skull, once the property of the late Luke Pratt, M.D." I don't quite know why I wrote that unless it was with the idea of explaining how the thing happened to be in my possession. I cannot help wondering sometimes what sort of hat it was that came in the bandbox. What color was it, do you think? Was it a cheery spring hat with a bobbing feather and pretty ribbons? Strange that the very same box should hold the head that wore the finery— perhaps. No—we made up our minds that it just came from the hospital in London where Luke did his time. It's far better to look at it in that light, isn't it? There's no more connection between that skull and poor Mrs. Pratt than there was between my story about the lead and—

Good Lord! Take the lamp—don't let it go out, if you can help it—I'll have the window fastened again in a second— I say, what a gale! There, it's out! I told you so! Never mind, there's the firelight—I've got the window shut—the bolt was only half down. Was the box blown off the table? Where the deuce is it? There! That won't open again, for I've put up the bar. Good dodge, an old-fashioned bar—there's nothing like it. Now, you find the bandbox while I light the lamp. Confound those wretched matches! Yes, a pipe spill is better—it must light in the fire—hadn't thought of it—thank you—there we are again. Now, where's the box? Yes, put it back on the table, and we'll open it.

That's the first time I have ever known the wind to burst that window open; but it was partly carelessness on my part when I last shut it. Yes, of course I heard the scream. It seemed to go all round the house before it broke in at the window. That proves that it's always been the wind and nothing else, doesn't it? When it was not the wind, it was my imagination. I've always been a very imaginative man: I must have been, though I did not know it. As we grow older we understand ourselves better, don't you know?

I'll have a drop of the Hulstkamp neat, by way of an exception, since you are filling up your glass. That damp gust chilled me, and with my rheumatic tendency I'm very much afraid of a chill, for the cold sometimes seems to stick in my joints all winter when it once gets in.

By george, that's good stuff! I'll just light a fresh pipe now that everything is snug again, and then we'll open the box. I'm so glad we heard that last scream together with the skull here on the table between us, for a thing cannot possibly be in two places at the same time, and the noise most certainly came from outside as any noise the wind makes must. You thought you heard it scream through the room after the window was burst open? Oh yes, so did I, but that was natural enough when everything was open. Of course we heard the wind. What could one expect?

Look here, please. I want you to see that the seal is intact before we open the box together. Will you take my glasses? No, you have your own. All right. The seal is sound, you see, and you can read the words of the motto easily. "Sweet and low"—that's it—because the poem goes on "Wind of the Western Sea," and says, "blow him again to me," and all that. Here is the seal on my watch chain where it's hung for more than 40 years. My poor little wife gave it to me when I was courting, and I never had any other. It was just like her to think of those words—she was always fond of Tennyson.

It's no use to cut the string, for it's fastened to the box, so I'll just break the wax and untie the knot, and afterward we'll seal it up again. You see, I like to feel that the thing is safe in its place, and that nobody can take it out. Not that I should suspect Trehearn of meddling with it, but I always feel that he knows a lot more than he tells.

You see, I've managed it without breaking the string, though when I fastened it I never expected to open the bandbox again. The lid comes off easily enough. There! Now look!

What! Nothing in it! Empty! It's gone, man, the skull is gone!

No, there's nothing the matter with me. I'm only trying to collect my thoughts. It's so strange. I'm positively certain that it was inside when I put on the seal last spring. I can't have imagined that: it's utterly impossible. If I ever took a stiff glass with a friend now and then, I would admit that I might have made some idiotic mistake when I had taken too much. But I don't, and I never did. A pint of ale at supper and half a go of rum at bedtime was the most I ever took in my good days. I believe it's always we sober fellows who get rheumatism and gout! Yet there was my seal, and there is the empty bandbox. That's plain enough.

I say, I don't half like this. It's not right. There's something wrong about it in my opinion. You needn't talk to me about supernatural manifestations, for I don't believe in them, not a little bit! Somebody must have tampered with the seal and stolen the skull. Sometimes when I go out to work in the garden in summer, I leave my watch and chain on the table. Trehearn must have taken the seal then, and used it, for he would be quite sure that I should not come in for at least an hour.

If it was not Trehearn—oh, don't talk to me about the possibility that the thing has got out by itself! If it has, it must be somewhere about the house in some out-of-the-way corner, waiting. We may come upon it anywhere, waiting for us, don't you know?—just waiting in the dark. Then it will scream at me; it will shriek at me in the dark, for it hates me, I tell you!

The bandbox is quite empty. We are not dreaming, either of us. There, I turn it upside down.

What's that? Something fell out as I turned it over. It's on the floor, it's near your feet. I know it is, and we must find it. Help me to find it, man. Have you got it? For God's sake, give it to me, quickly!

Lead! I knew it when I heard it fall. I knew it couldn't be anything else by the little thud it made on the hearthrug. So it was lead after all, and Luke did it.

I feel a little bit shaken up—not exactly nervous, you know, but badly shaken up, that's the fact. Anybody would, I should think. After all, you cannot say that it's fear of the thing, for I went up and brought it down—at least, I believed

65

I was bringing it down, and that's the same thing, and by george, rather than give in to such silly nonsense, I'll take the box upstairs again and put it back in its place. It's not that. It's the certainty that the poor little woman came to her end in that way, by my fault, because I told the story. That's what is so dreadful. Somehow, I had always hoped that I should never be quite sure of it, but there is no doubting it now. Look at that!

Look at it! That little lump of lead with no particular shape. Think of what it did, man! Doesn't it make you shiver? He gave her something to make her sleep, of course, but there must have been one moment of awful agony. Think of having boiling lead poured into your brain. Think of it. She was dead before she could scream, but only think of—oh! there it is again—it's just outside—I know it's just outside—I can't keep it out of my head!—oh!—oh!

❦

You thought I had fainted? No, I wish I had, for it would have stopped sooner. It's all very well to say that it's only a noise, and that a noise never hurt anybody—you're as white as a shroud yourself. There's only one thing to be done, if we hope to close an eye tonight. We must find it and put it back into its bandbox and shut it up in the cupboard where it likes to be. I don't know how it got out, but it wants to get in again. That's why it screams so awfully tonight—it was never so bad as this—never since I first—

Bury it? Yes, if we can find it, we'll bury it, if it takes us all night. We'll bury it six feet deep and ram down the earth over it so that it shall never get out again, and if it screams, we shall hardly hear it so deep down. Quick, we'll get the lantern and look for it. It cannot be far away; I'm

66

sure it's just outside—it was coming in when I shut the window, I know it.

Yes, you're quite right. I'm losing my senses, and I must get hold of myself. Don't speak to me for a minute or two; I'll sit quite still and keep my eyes shut and repeat something I know. That's the best way.

"Add together the altitude, the latitude, and the polar distance, divide by two and subtract the altitude from the half-sum; then add the logarithm of the secant of the latitude, the cosecant of the polar distance, the cosine of the half-sum and the sine of the half-sum minus the altitude"—there! Don't say that I'm out of my senses, for my memory is all right, isn't it?

Of course, you may say that it's mechanical, and that we never forget the things we learned when we were boys and have used almost every day for a lifetime. But that's the very point. When a man is going crazy, it's the mechanical part of his mind that gets out of order and won't work right; he remembers things that never happened, or he sees things that aren't real, or he hears noises when there is perfect silence. That's not what is the matter with either of us, is it?

Come, we'll get the lantern and go round the house. It's not raining—only blowing like old boots, as we used to say. The lantern is in the cupboard under the stairs in the hall, and I always keep it trimmed in case of a wreck.

No use to look for the thing? I don't see how you can say that. It was nonsense to talk of burying it, of course, for it doesn't want to be buried; it wants to go back into its bandbox and be taken upstairs, poor thing! Trehearn took it out, I know, and made the seal over again. Perhaps he took it to the churchyard, and he may have meant well. I dare say he thought that it would not scream any more if it were quietly laid in consecrated ground near where it belongs. But it has

67

come home. Yes, that's it. He's not half a bad fellow, Trehearn, and rather religiously inclined, I think. Does not that sound natural, and reasonable, and well meant? He supposed it screamed because it was not decently buried—with the rest. But he was wrong. How should he know that it screams at me because it hates me, and because it's my fault that there was that little lump of lead in it?

No use to look for it, anyhow? Nonsense! I tell you it wants to be found—Hark! what's that knocking? Do you hear it? Knock—knock—knock—three times, then a pause, and then again. It has a hollow sound, hasn't it?

It has come home. I've heard that knock before. It wants to come in and be taken upstairs in its box. It's at the front door.

Will you come with me? We'll take it in. Yes, I own that I don't like to go alone and open the door. The thing will roll in and stop against my foot just as it did before, and the light will go out. I'm a good deal shaken by finding that bit of lead, and besides my heart isn't quite right—too much strong tobacco, perhaps. Besides, I'm quite willing to own that I'm a bit nervous tonight, if I never was before in my life.

That's right, come along! I'll take the box with me so as not to come back. Do you hear the knocking? It's not like any other knocking I ever heard. If you will hold this door open, I can find the lantern under the stairs by the light from this room without bringing the lamp into the hall—it would only go out.

The thing knows we are coming—hark! It's impatient to get in. Don't shut the door till the lantern is ready, whatever you do. There will be the usual trouble with the matches, I suppose—no, the first one, by Jove! I tell you it wants to get in so there's no trouble. All right with that door now; shut it, please. Now come and hold the lantern, for it's blowing so hard outside that I shall have to use both hands. That's it, hold the light low. Do you hear the knocking still? Here goes—I'll open just enough with my foot against the bottom of the door—now!

Catch it! It's only the wind that blows it across the floor, that's all—there's half a hurricane outside, I tell you! Have you got it? The bandbox is on the table. One minute, and I'll have the bar up. There!

Why did you throw it into the box so roughly? It doesn't like that, you know.

What do you say? Bitten your hand? Nonsense, man! You did just what I did. You pressed the jaws together with your other hand and pinched yourself. Let me see. You don't mean to say you have drawn blood? You must have squeezed hard, by Jove, for the skin is certainly torn. I'll give you some carbolic solution for it before we go to bed, for they say a scratch from a skull's tooth may go bad and give trouble.

Come inside again and let me see it by the lamp. I'll bring the bandbox—never mind the lantern, it may just as well burn in the hall, for I shall need it presently when I go up the stairs. Yes, shut the door if you will; it makes it more cheerful and bright. Is your finger still bleeding? I'll get you the carbolic in an instant; just let me see the thing.

Ugh! There's a drop of blood on the upper jaw. It's on the eyetooth. Ghastly, isn't it? When I saw it running along the floor of the hall, the strength almost went out of my hands, and I felt my knees bending, then I understood that it was the gale driving it over the smooth boards. You don't blame me? No, I should think not! We were boys together, and we've seen a thing or two, and we may just as well own to each other that we were both in a beastly funk when it slid across the floor at you. No wonder you pinched your finger picking it up, after that, if I did the same thing out of sheer nervousness in broad daylight with the sun streaming in on me.

Strange that the jaw should stick to it so closely, isn't it? I suppose it's the dampness, for it shuts like a vise—I have wiped off the drop of blood, for it was not nice to look at. I'm not going to try to open the jaws, don't be afraid! I shall not play any tricks with the poor thing, but I'll just seal the box again, and we'll take it upstairs and put it away where it wants to be.

The wax is on the writing table by the window. Thank you. It will be long before I leave my seal lying about again, for Trehearn to use, I can tell you. Explain? I don't explain natural phenomena, but if you choose to think that Trehearn had hidden it somewhere in the bushes, and that the gale blew it to the house against the door and made it knock as if it wanted to be let in, you're not thinking the impossible, and I'm quite ready to agree with you.

Do you see that? You can swear that you've actually seen me seal it this time in case anything of the kind should occur again. The wax fastens the strings to the lid, which cannot possibly be lifted even enough to get in one finger. You're quite satisfied, aren't you? Yes. Besides, I shall lock the cupboard and keep the key in my pocket hereafter.

Now we can take the lantern and go upstairs. Do you know? I'm very much inclined to agree with your theory that the wind blew it against the house. I'll go ahead, for I know the stairs; just hold the lantern near my feet as we go up. How the wind howls and whistles! Did you feel the sand on the floor under your shoes as we crossed the hall?

Yes—this is the door of the best bedroom. Hold up the lantern, please. This side, by the head of the bed. I left the cupboard open when I got the box. Isn't it odd how the faint odor of women's dresses will hang about an old closet for years? This is the shelf. You've seen me set the box there, and now you see me turn the key and put it into my pocket. So that's done!

Goodnight. Are you sure you're quite comfortable? It's not much of a room, but I dare say you would as soon sleep here as upstairs tonight. If you want anything, sing out; there's only a lath and plaster partition between us. There's not so much wind on this side by half. There's the Hollands on the table, if you'll have one more nightcap. No? Well, do as you please. Goodnight again, and don't dream about that thing, if you can.

❧

The following paragraph appeared in the *Penraddon News*, 23rd November 1906:

MYSTERIOUS DEATH OF A RETIRED SEA CAPTAIN

The village of Tredcombe is much disturbed by the strange death of Captain Charles Braddock, and all sorts of impossible stories are circulating with regard to the circumstances which certainly seem difficult of explanation. The retired captain, who had successfully commanded in his time the largest and fastest liners belonging to one of the principal transatlantic steamship companies, was found dead in his bed on Tuesday morning in his own cottage, a quarter of a mile from the village. An examination was made at once by the local practitioner which revealed the horrible fact that the deceased had been bitten in the throat by a human assailant with such amazing force as to crush the windpipe and cause death. The marks of the teeth of both jaws were so plainly visible on the skin that they could be counted, but the perpetrator of the deed had evidently lost the two lower middle incisors. It is hoped that this peculiarity may help to identify the murderer, who can only be a dangerous escaped maniac.

The deceased, though over 65 years of age, is said to have been a hale man of considerable physical strength, and it is remarkable that no signs of any struggle were visible in the room, nor could it be ascertained how the murderer had entered the house. Warning has been sent to all the insane asylums in the United Kingdom, but as yet no information has been received regarding the escape of any dangerous patient.

The coroner's jury returned the somewhat singular verdict that Captain Braddock came to his death "by the hands or teeth of some person unknown." The local surgeon is said to have expressed privately the opinion that the maniac is a woman, a view he deduces from the small size of the jaws as shown by the marks of the teeth. The whole affair is shrouded in mystery. Captain Braddock was a widower and lived alone. He leaves no children.

MAN-SIZE IN MARBLE (1893)

by

Edith Nesbit

(1858–1924)

Edith Nesbit *was born in England, but was educated in convents both in England and in Europe. In 1880 she married Hubert Bland. She and her husband were founding members of the Fabian Society, a group that aimed to spread socialist ideals among educated citizens. Although Nesbit enjoyed writing poetry most of all, her marriage turned stormy and she had to support herself and four children by writing stories and novels.*

Nesbit is best remembered for her children's novels, such as Five Children and It *(1902),* The Phoenix and the Carpet *(1904),* The Railway Children *(1906), and* The Enchanted Castle *(1907), many of which are now being reprinted. She also wrote a great deal of popular fiction, including many ghost stories.*

In the following tale, a young man makes light of an old woman's warnings about strange events soon to come. Too late he learns what folly it is to ignore those wiser and more experienced than he.

ALTHOUGH EVERY WORD OF THIS STORY IS AS TRUE AS despair, I do not expect people to believe it. Nowadays a rational explanation is required before belief is possible. Let me then at once offer the rational explanation which finds most favor among those who have heard the tale of my life's tragedy. It is held that we were under a delusion, Laura and I, on that 31st of October; and that this supposition places the

73

whole matter on a satisfactory and believable basis. The reader can judge, when he, too, has heard my story, how far this is an explanation, and in what sense it is rational. There were three who took part in this: Laura and I and another man. The other man still lives, and can speak to the truth of the least credible part of my story.

I never in my life knew what it was to have as much money as I required to supply the most ordinary needs—good colors, books, and cab fares—and when we were married, we knew quite well that we should only be able to live at all by strict punctuality and attention to business. I used to paint in those days, and Laura used to write, and we felt sure we could keep the pot at least simmering.

Living in town was out of the question, so we went to look for a cottage in the country, which should be at once sanitary and picturesque. So rarely do these two qualities meet in one cottage that our search was for some time quite fruitless. We tried advertisements, but most of the desirable rural residences which we did look at proved to be lacking in both essentials, and when a cottage chanced to have drains, it always had stucco as well and was shaped like a tea caddy. And if we found a vine- or rose-covered porch, corruption invariably lurked within. Our minds got so befogged by the eloquence of house agents and the rival disadvantages of the fever traps and outrages to beauty which we had seen and scorned, that I very much doubt whether either of us, on our wedding morning, knew the difference between a house and a haystack.

But when we got away from friends and house agents, on our honeymoon, our wits grew clear again, and we knew a pretty cottage when at last we saw one. It was at Brenzett—a little village set on a hill over against the southern marshes. We had gone there, from the seaside village where we were staying, to see the church, and two fields from the church we found this cottage.

It stood quite by itself, about two miles from the village. It was a long, low building, with rooms sticking out in unexpected places. There was a bit of stonework—ivy-covered and moss-grown, just two old rooms, all that was left of a big house that had once stood there—and round this stonework the house had grown up. Stripped of its roses and jasmine it would have been hideous. As it stood it was charming, and after a brief examination we took it. It was absurdly cheap.

The rest of our honeymoon we spent in grubbing about in secondhand shops in the county town, picking up bits of old oak and Chippendale chairs for our furnishing. We wound up with a run up to town and a visit to Liberty's, and soon the low oak-beamed lattice-windowed rooms began to be home. There was a jolly old-fashioned garden, with grass paths and no end of hollyhocks and sunflowers and big lilies. From the window you could see the marsh pastures and beyond them the blue, thin line of the sea.

We were as happy as the summer was glorious and settled down into work sooner than we ourselves expected. I was never tired of sketching the view and the wonderful cloud effects from the open lattice, and Laura would sit at the table and write verses about them in which I mostly played the part of foreground.

We got a tall old peasant woman to do for us. Her face and figure were good, though her cooking was of the homeliest; but she understood all about gardening and told us all the old names of the coppices and cornfields, and the stories of the smugglers and highwaymen and, better still, of the things that walked, and of the sights which met one in lonely glens of a starlight night. She was a great comfort to us, because Laura hated housekeeping as much as I loved folklore, and we soon came to leave all the domestic business to Mrs. Dorman, and to use her legends in little magazine stories which brought in the jingling guinea.

We had three months of married happiness, and did not have a single quarrel. One October evening I had been down to smoke a pipe with the doctor—our only neighbor—a pleasant young Irishman. Laura had stayed at home to finish a comic sketch of a village episode for the *Monthly Marplot.* I left her laughing over her own jokes, and came in to find her a crumpled heap of pale muslin weeping on the window seat.

"Good heavens, my darling, what's the matter?" I cried, taking her in my arms. She leaned her little dark head against my shoulder and went on crying. I had never seen her cry before—we had always been so happy, you see—and I felt sure some frightful misfortune had happened.

"What is the matter? Do speak."

"It's Mrs. Dorman," she sobbed.

"What has she done?" I inquired, immensely relieved.

"She says she must go before the end of the month, and she says her niece is ill; she's gone down to see her now, but I don't believe that's the reason, because her niece is always ill. I believe someone has been setting her against us. Her manner was so strange—"

"Never mind, dear," I said; "whatever you do, don't cry, or I shall have to cry too, to keep you in countenance, and then you'll never respect your man again!"

She dried her eyes obediently on my handkerchief, and even smiled faintly.

"But you see," she went on, "it is really serious, because these village people are so sheepy, and if one won't do a thing, you may be quite sure none of the others will.

And I shall have to cook the dinners, and wash up the hateful greasy plates; and you'll have to carry cans of water about, and clean the boots and knives—and we shall never have any time for work, or earn any money, or anything. We shall have to work all day, and only be able to rest when we are waiting for the kettle to boil!"

I represented to her that even if we had to perform these duties the day would still present some margin for other toils and recreations. But she refused to see the matter in any but the grayest light. She was very unreasonable, my Laura, but I could not have loved her any more if she had been as reasonable as Whately.

"I'll speak to Mrs. Dorman when she comes back, and see if I can't come to terms with her," I said. "Perhaps she wants a rise in her screw. It will be all right. Let's walk up to the church."

The church was a large and lonely one, and we loved to go there, especially upon bright nights. The path skirted a wood, cut through it once, and ran along the crest of the hill through two meadows and round the churchyard wall, over which the old yews loomed in black masses of shadow. This path, which was partly paved, was called the bier-balk, for it had long been the way by which the corpses had been carried to burial. The churchyard was richly treed, and was shaded by great elms which stood just outside and stretched their majestic arms in benediction over the happy dead.

A large, low porch let one into the building by a Norman doorway and a heavy oak door studded with iron. Inside, the arches rose into darkness, and between them the reticulated windows, which stood out white in the moonlight. In the chancel, the windows were of rich glass, which showed in faint light their noble coloring, and made the black oak of the choir pews hardly more solid than the shadows.

But on each side of the altar lay a gray marble figure of a knight in full plate armor lying upon a low slab, with hands held up in everlasting prayer, and these figures, oddly enough, were always to be seen if there was any glimmer of light in the church. Their names were lost, but the peasants told of them that they had been fierce and wicked men, marauders by land and sea, who had been the scourge of their time, and had been guilty of deeds so foul that the house they had lived in—the big house, by the way, that had stood on the site of our cottage—had been stricken by lightning and the vengeance of heaven. But for all that, the gold of their heirs had bought them a place in the church. Looking at the bad hard faces reproduced in the marble, this story was easily believed.

The church looked at its best and weirdest on that night, for the shadows of the yew trees fell through the windows upon the floor of the nave and touched the pillars with tattered shade. We sat down together without speaking and watched the solemn beauty of the old church with some of that awe which inspired its early builders. We walked to the chancel and looked at the sleeping warriors. Then we rested some time on the stone seat in the porch, looking out over the stretch of quiet moonlit meadows, feeling in every fiber of our being the peace of the night and of our happy love; and came away at last with a sense that even scrubbing and blackleading were but small troubles at their worst.

Mrs. Dorman had come back from the village, and I at once invited her to a tête-à-tête.

"Now, Mrs. Dorman," I said, when I had got her into my painting room, "what's all this about your not staying with us?"

"I should be glad to get away, sir, before the end of the month," she answered, with her usual placid dignity.

"Have you any fault to find, Mrs. Dorman?"

"None at all, sir; you and your lady have always been most kind, I'm sure—"

"Well, what is it? Are your wages not high enough?"

"No, sir, I gets quite enough."

"Then why not stay?"

"I'd rather not"—with some hesitation—"my niece is ill."

"But your niece has been ill ever since we came."

No answer. There was a long and awkward silence. I broke it.

"Can't you stay for another month?" I asked.

"No, sir. I'm bound to go by Thursday."

And this was Monday!

"Well, I must say, I think you might have let us know before. There's no time now to get any one else, and your mistress is not fit to do heavy housework. Can't you stay till next week?"

"I might be able to come back next week."

I was now convinced that all she wanted was a brief holiday, which we should have been willing enough to let her have as soon as we could get a substitute.

"But why must you go this week?" I persisted. "Come, out with it."

Mrs. Dorman drew the little shawl which she always wore tightly across her bosom as though she were cold. Then she said, with a sort of effort—

"They say, sir, as this was a big house in Catholic times, and there was a many deeds done here."

The nature of the "deeds" might be vaguely inferred from the inflection of Mrs. Dorman's voice—which was enough to make one's blood run cold. I was glad that Laura was not in the room. She was always nervous, as highly strung natures are, and I felt that these tales about our house, told by this old peasant woman, with her impressive manner and contagious credulity might have made our home less dear to my wife.

"Tell me all about it, Mrs. Dorman," I said, "you needn't mind about telling me. I'm not like the young people who make fun of such things."

Which was partly true.

"Well, sir"—she sank her voice—"you may have seen in the church, beside the altar, two shapes."

"You mean the effigies of the knights in armor," I said cheerfully.

"I mean them two bodies, drawed out man-size in marble," she returned, and I had to admit that her description was a thousand times more graphic than mine, to say nothing of a certain weird force and uncanniness about the phrase "drawed out man-size in marble."

"They do say, as on All Saints' Eve them two bodies sits up on their slabs and gets off of them and then walks down the aisle in their marble"—(another good phrase, Mrs. Dorman)—"and as the church clock strikes eleven they walks out of the church door and over the graves and along the bier-balk, and if it's a wet night there's the marks of their feet in the morning."

"And where do they go?" I asked, rather fascinated.

"They comes back here to their home, sir, and if any one meets them—"

"Well, what then?" I asked.

But no—not another word could I get from her save that her niece was ill and she must go. After what I had heard, I scorned to discuss the niece and tried to get from Mrs. Dorman more details of the legend. I could get nothing but warnings.

"Whatever you do, sir, lock the door early on All Saints' Eve, and make the cross sign over the doorstep and on the windows."

"But has any one ever seen these things?" I persisted.

"That's not for me to say. I know what I know, sir."

"Well, who was here last year?"

"No one, sir; the lady as owned the house only stayed here in summer, and she always went to London a full month afore the night. And I'm sorry to inconvenience you and your lady, but my niece is ill and I must go on Thursday."

I could have shaken her for her absurd reiteration of that obvious fiction after she had told me her real reasons.

She was determined to go, nor could our united entreaties move her in the least.

I did not tell Laura the legend of the shapes that "walked in their marble," partly because a legend concerning our house might perhaps trouble my wife, and partly, I think, from some more occult reason. This was not quite the same to me as any other story, and I did not want to talk about it till the day was over. I had very soon ceased to think of the legend, however. I was painting a portrait of Laura, against the lattice window, and I could not think of much else. I had got a splendid background of yellow and gray sunset, and was working away with enthusiasm at her lace. On Thursday Mrs. Dorman went. She relented, at parting, so far as to say—

"Don't you put yourself about too much, ma'am, and if there's any little thing I can do next week I'm sure I shan't mind."

From which I inferred that she wished to come back to us after Halloween. Up to the last she adhered to the fiction of the niece with touching fidelity.

81

Thursday passed off pretty well. Laura showed marked ability in the matter of steak and potatoes, and I confess that my knives and the plates, which I insisted upon washing, were better done than I had dared to expect.

Friday came. It is about what happened on that Friday that this is written. I wonder if I should have believed it if any one had told it to me. I will write the story of it as quickly and plainly as I can. Everything that happened on that day is burnt into my brain. I shall not forget anything, nor leave anything out.

I got up early, I remember, and lighted the kitchen fire, and had just achieved a smoky success when my little wife came running down as sunny and sweet as the clear October morning itself. We prepared breakfast together and found it very good fun. The housework was soon done, and when brushes and brooms and pails were quiet again the house was still indeed. It is wonderful what a difference one makes in a house. We really missed Mrs. Dorman, quite apart from considerations concerning pots and pans. We spent the day in dusting our books and putting them straight and dined gaily on cold steak and coffee. Laura was, if possible, brighter and gayer and sweeter than usual, and I began to think that a little domestic toil was really good for her. We had never been so merry since we were married, and the walk we had that afternoon was, I think, the happiest time of all my life. When we had watched the deep scarlet clouds slowly pale into leaden gray against a pale green sky and saw the white mists curl up along the hedgerows in the distant marsh, we came back to the house, silently, hand in hand.

"You are sad, my darling," I said, half-jestingly, as we sat down together in our little parlor. I expected a disclaimer, for my own silence had been the silence of complete happiness. To my surprise she said—

"Yes. I think I am sad, or rather I am uneasy. I don't think I'm very well. I have shivered three or four times since we came in, and it is not cold, is it?"

"No," I said, and hoped it was not a chill caught from the treacherous mists that roll up from the marshes in the dying light. No—she said, she did not think so. Then, after a silence, she spoke suddenly—

"Do you ever have presentiments of evil?"

"No," I said, smiling, "and I shouldn't believe in them if I had."

"I do," she went on; "the night my father died I knew it, though he was right away in the north of Scotland." I did not answer in words.

She sat looking at the fire for some time in silence, gently stroking my hand. At last she sprang up, came behind me, and, drawing my head back, kissed me.

"There, it's over now," she said. "What a baby I am! Come, light the candles, and we'll have some of these new Rubinstein duets."

And we spent a happy hour or two at the piano.

At about half-past ten I began to long for the good-night pipe, but Laura looked so white that I felt it would be brutal of me to fill our sitting room with the fumes of strong tobacco.

"I'll take my pipe outside," I said.

"Let me come, too."

"No, sweetheart, not tonight; you're much too tired. I shan't be long. Get to bed, or I shall have an invalid to nurse tomorrow as well as the boots to clean."

I kissed her and was turning to go, when she flung her arms round my neck, and held me as if she would never let me go again. I stroked her hair.

"Come, dear, you're overtired. The housework has been too much for you."

She loosened her clasp a little and drew a deep breath.

"No. We've been very happy today, Jack, haven't we? Don't stay out too long."

"I won't, my dearie."

I strolled out of the front door, leaving it unlatched. What a night it was! The jagged masses of heavy dark clouds were rolling at intervals from horizon to horizon, and thin white wreaths covered the stars. Through all the rush of the cloud river the moon swam, breasting the waves and disappearing again in the darkness. When now and again her light reached the woodlands they seemed to be slowly and noiselessly waving in time to the swing of the clouds above them. There was a strange gray light over all the earth; the fields had that shadowy bloom over them which only comes from the marriage of dew and moonshine, or frost and starlight.

I walked up and down, drinking in the beauty of the quiet earth and the changing sky. The night was absolutely silent. Nothing seemed to be abroad. There was no scurrying of rabbits, or twitter of the half-asleep birds. And though the clouds went sailing across the sky, the wind that drove them never came low enough to rustle the dead leaves in the woodland paths. Across the meadows I could see the church tower standing out black and gray against the sky. I walked there thinking over our three months of happiness—and of my wife, her dear eyes, her loving ways. Oh, my little girl! my own little girl; what a vision came then of a long, glad life for you and me together!

I heard a bell beat from the church. Eleven already! I turned to go in, but the night held me. I could not go back into our little warm rooms yet. I would go up to the church. I felt vaguely that it would be good to carry my love and thankfulness to the sanctuary whither so many loads of sorrow and gladness had been borne by the men and women of the dead years.

I looked in at the low window as I went by. Laura was half lying on her chair in front of the fire. I could not see her face, only her little head showed dark against the pale blue wall. She was quite still. Asleep, no doubt. My heart reached out to her, as I went on. There must be a God, I thought, and a God who was good. How otherwise could anything so sweet and dear as she have ever been imagined?

I walked slowly along the edge of the wood. A sound broke the stillness of the night, it was a rustling in the wood. I stopped and listened. The sound stopped too. I went on, and now distinctly heard another step than mine answer mine like an echo. It was a poacher or a wood stealer, most likely, for these were not unknown in our Arcadian neighborhood. But whoever it was, he was a fool not to step more lightly. I turned into the wood, and now the footstep seemed to come from the path I had just left. It must be an echo, I thought.

The wood looked perfect in the moonlight. The large dying ferns and the brushwood showed where through thinning foliage the pale light came down. The tree trunks stood up like Gothic columns all around me. They reminded me of the church, and I turned into the bier-balk, and passed through the corpse gate between the graves to the low porch. I paused for a moment on the stone seat where Laura and I had watched the fading landscape.

Then I noticed that the door of the church was open, and I blamed myself for having left it unlatched the other night. We were the only people who ever cared to come to the church except on Sundays, and I was vexed to think that through our carelessness the damp autumn airs had had a chance of getting in and injuring the old fabric. I went in. It will seem strange, perhaps, that I should have gone halfway up the aisle before I remembered—with a sudden chill, followed by as sudden a rush of self-contempt—that this was the very day and hour when, according to tradition, the shapes drawed out man-size in marble began to walk.

Having thus remembered the legend, and remembered it with a shiver, of which I was ashamed, I could not do otherwise than walk up toward the altar just to look at the figures—as I said to myself; really what I wanted was to assure myself, first, that I did not believe the legend and, secondly, that it was not true. I was rather glad that I had come. I thought now I could tell Mrs. Dorman how vain her fancies were and how peacefully the marble figures slept on through the ghastly hour. With my hands in my pockets I passed up the aisle. In the gray dim light the eastern end of the church looked larger than usual, and the arches above the two tombs looked larger too. The moon came out and showed me the reason. I stopped short, my heart gave a leap that nearly choked me, and then sank sickeningly.

The bodies drawed out man-size were gone, and their marble slabs lay wide and bare in the vague moonlight that slanted through the east window.

Were they really gone? or was I mad? Clenching my nerves, I stooped and passed my hand over the smooth slabs, and felt their flat unbroken surface. Had someone taken the things away? Was it some vile practical joke? I would make sure, anyway. In an instant I had made a torch of a newspaper, which happened to be in my pocket, and lighting it held it high above my head. Its yellow glare illumined the dark arches and those slabs. The figures were gone. And I was alone in the church; or was I alone?

And then a horror seized me, a horror indefinable and indescribable—an overwhelming certainty of supreme and accomplished calamity. I flung down the torch and tore along the aisle and out through the porch, biting my lips as I ran to keep myself from shrieking aloud. Oh, was I mad—or what was this that possessed me? I leaped the churchyard wall and took the straight cut across the fields, led by the light from our windows. Just as I got over the first stile, a dark figure seemed to spring out of the ground. Mad still with that certainty of misfortune, I made for the thing that stood in my path, shouting, "Get out of the way, can't you!"

But my push met with a more vigorous resistance than I had expected. My arms were caught just above the elbow and held as in a vise, and the rawboned Irish doctor actually shook me.

"Would ye?" he cried, in his own unmistakable accents—"would ye, then?"

"Let me go, you fool," I gasped. "The marble figures have gone from the church; I tell you they've gone."

He broke into a ringing laugh. "I'll have to give ye a draught tomorrow, I see. Ye've bin smoking too much and listening to old wives' tales."

"I tell you, I've seen the bare slabs."

"Well, come back with me. I'm going up to old Palmer's—his daughter's ill; we'll look in at the church and let me see the bare slabs."

"You go, if you like," I said, a little less frantic for his laughter; "I'm going home to my wife."

"Rubbish, man," said he; "d'ye think I'll permit of that? Are ye to go saying all yer life that ye've seen solid marble endowed with vitality, and me to go all me life saying ye were a coward? No, sir—ye shan't do it."

The night air—a human voice—and I think also the physical contact with this six feet of solid common sense, brought me back a little to my ordinary self, and the word "coward" was a mental shower bath.

"Come on, then," I said sullenly; "perhaps you're right."

He still held my arm tightly. We got over the stile and back to the church. All was still as death. The place smelt very damp and earthy. We walked up the aisle. I am not ashamed to confess that I shut my eyes: I knew the figures would not be there. I heard Kelly strike a match.

"Here they are, ye see, right enough; ye've been dreaming or drinking, asking yer pardon for the imputation."

I opened my eyes. By Kelly's expiring vesta I saw two shapes lying in their marble on their slabs. I drew a deep breath, and caught his hand.

"I'm awfully indebted to you," I said. "It must have been some trick of light, or I have been working rather hard, perhaps that's it. Do you know, I was quite convinced they were gone."

"I'm aware of that," he answered rather grimly; "ye'll have to be careful of that brain of yours, my friend, I assure ye."

He was leaning over and looking at the right-hand figure, whose stony face was the most villainous and deadly in expression.

"By Jove," he said, "something has been afoot here—this hand is broken."

And so it was. I was certain that it had been perfect the last time Laura and I had been there.

"Perhaps some one has tried to remove them," said the young doctor.

"That won't account for my impression," I objected.

"Too much painting and tobacco will account for that, well enough."

"Come along," I said, "or my wife will be getting anxious. You'll come in and have a drop of whisky and drink confusion to ghosts and better sense to me."

"I ought to go up to Palmer's, but it's so late now I'd best leave it till the morning," he replied. "I was kept late at the Union, and I've had to see a lot of people since. All right, I'll come back with ye."

I think he fancied I needed him more than did Palmer's girl, so, discussing how such an illusion could have been possible and deducing from this experience large generalities concerning ghostly apparitions, we walked up to our cottage. We saw, as we walked up the garden path, that bright light streamed out of the front door and presently saw that the parlor door was open too. Had she gone out?

"Come in," I said, and Dr. Kelly followed me into the parlor. It was all ablaze with candles, not only the wax ones, but at least a dozen guttering, glaring tallow dips, stuck in vases and ornaments in unlikely places. Light, I knew, was Laura's remedy for nervousness. Poor child! Why had I left her? Brute that I was.

We glanced round the room, and at first we did not see her. The window was open, and the draught set all the candles flaring one way. Her chair was empty and her handkerchief and book lay on the floor. I turned to the window. There, in the recess of the window, I saw her. Oh, my child, my love, had she gone to that window to watch for me? And what had come into the room behind her? To what had she turned with that look of frantic fear and horror? Oh, my little one, had she thought that it was I whose step she heard, and turned to meet—what?

She had fallen back across a table in the window, and her body lay half on it and half on the window-seat, and her head hung down over the table, the brown hair loosened and fallen to the carpet. Her lips were drawn back, and her eyes wide, wide open. They saw nothing now. What had they seen last?

89

The doctor moved toward her, but I pushed him aside and sprang to her; caught her in my arms and cried—

"It's all right, Laura! I've got you safe, wifie."

She fell into my arms in a heap. I clasped her and kissed her, and called her by all her pet names, but I think I knew all the time that she was dead. Her hands were tightly clenched. In one of them she held something fast. When I was quite sure that she was dead and that nothing mattered at all anymore, I let him open her hand to see what she held.

It was a gray marble finger.

THE RING OF THOTH (1890)

by

Sir Arthur Conan Doyle

(1859–1930)

Sir Arthur Conan Doyle *published his first story, "The Mystery of Sasassa Valley," in 1879 while serving as a medical assistant to a doctor in Birmingham, England. He had written tales for the doctor's children and was noted by his companions for his lively and vivid letters. Friends urged him to submit his stories to magazines. Encouraged by his subsequent success, Conan Doyle went on to a long and illustrious writing career.*

While Conan Doyle is most famous for his Sherlock Holmes stories, these were the stories he liked the least. He wanted to be remembered for his well-researched historical novels, such as The White Company *and* Micah Clarke. *He also wrote many tales of adventure, including the Professor Challenger stories ("The Lost World" and "The Poison Belt").*

Conan Doyle was a highly educated man, whose vast store of knowledge spills out into this tale of ancient Egyptian intrigue. We begin with a highly gifted young man who travels to the Louvre in Paris to study ancient Egyptian artifacts—only to discover that the most fascinating antiquity there is still very much alive.

MR. JOHN VANSITTART SMITH, F.R.S., OF 147A GOWER Street, was a man whose energy of purpose and clearness of thought might have placed him in the very first rank of scientific observers. He was the victim, however, of a universal ambition which prompted him to aim at distinction in many subjects rather than preeminence in one. In his early days he

92

had shown aptitude for zoology and for botany which caused his friends to look upon him as a second Darwin, but when a professorship was almost within his reach, he had suddenly discontinued his studies and turned his whole attention to chemistry. Here his researches upon the spectra of the metals had won him his fellowship in the Royal Society; but again he played the coquette with his subject, and after a year's absence from the laboratory he joined the Oriental Society, and delivered a paper on the hieroglyphic and demotic inscriptions of El Kab, thus giving a crowning example both of the versatility and of the inconstancy of his talents.

The most fickle of wooers, however, is apt to be caught at last, and so it was with John Vansittart Smith. The more he burrowed his way into Egyptology, the more impressed he became by the vast field which it opened to the inquirer, and by the extreme importance of a subject which promised to throw a light upon the first germs of human civilization and the origin of the greater part of our arts and sciences.

So struck was Mr. Smith that he straightway married an Egyptological young lady who had written upon the Sixth Dynasty, and having thus secured a sound base of operations, he set himself to collect materials for a work which should unite the research of Lepsius and the ingenuity of Champollion. The preparation of his magnum opus entailed many hurried visits to the magnificent Egyptian collections of the Louvre, upon the last of which, no longer ago than the middle of last October, he became involved in a most strange and noteworthy adventure.

The trains had been slow and the Channel had been rough, so that the student arrived in Paris in a somewhat befogged and feverish condition. On reaching the Hotel de France, in the Rue Laffitte, he had thrown himself upon a sofa for a couple of hours. Finding that he was unable to sleep, he determined in spite of his fatigue to make his way to the Louvre, settle the point which he had come to decide, and take the evening train back to Dieppe. Having come to his conclusion, he donned his greatcoat, for it was a raw rainy day, and made his way across the Boulevard des Italiens and down the Avenue de l'Opera. Once in the Louvre he was on familiar ground, and he speedily made his way to the collection of papyri which it was his intention to consult.

The warmest admirers of John Vansittart Smith could hardly claim for him that he was a handsome man. His high-beaked nose and prominent chin had something of the same acute and incisive character which distinguished his intellect. He held his head in a birdlike fashion, and birdlike, too, was the pecking motion with which in conversation he threw out his objections and retorts. As he stood with the high collar of his greatcoat raised to his ears, he might have seen from the reflection in the glass-case before him that his appearance was a singular one. Yet it came upon him as a sudden jar when an English voice behind him exclaimed in very audible tones, "What an odd-looking mortal!"

The student had a large amount of petty vanity in his personality which manifested itself by an ostentatious and overdone disregard of all personal considerations. He straightened his lips and looked rigidly at the roll of papyrus, while his heart filled with bitterness against the whole race of traveling Britons.

"Yes," said another voice, "he really is an extraordinary fellow."

"Do you know," said the first speaker, "one could almost believe that by the continual contemplation of mummies the chap has become half a mummy himself?"

"He has certainly an Egyptian cast of countenance," said the other.

John Vansittart Smith spun round upon his heel with the intention of shaming his countrymen by a corrosive remark or two. To his surprise and relief, the two young fellows who had been conversing had their shoulders turned toward him, and were gazing at one of the Louvre attendants who was polishing some brasswork at the other side of the room.

"Carter will be waiting for us at the Palais Royal," said one tourist to the other, glancing at his watch, and they clattered away, leaving the student to his labors.

"I wonder what these chatterers call an Egyptian cast of countenance," thought John Vansittart Smith, and he moved his position slightly in order to catch a glimpse of the man's face. He started as his eyes fell upon it. It was indeed the very face with which his studies had made him familiar. The regular statuesque features, broad brow, well-rounded chin, and dusky complexion were the exact counterpart of the innumerable statues, mummy cases, and pictures which adorned the walls of the apartment. The thing was beyond all coincidence. The man must be an Egyptian. The national angularity of the shoulders and narrowness of the hips were alone sufficient to identify him.

John Vansittart Smith shuffled toward the attendant with some intention of addressing him. He was not light of touch in conversation, and found it difficult to strike the happy mean between the brusqueness of the superior and the geniality of the equal. As he came nearer, the man presented his side face to him, but kept his gaze still bent upon his work. Vansittart Smith, fixing his eyes upon the fellow's skin, was conscious of a sudden impression that there was something inhuman and preternatural about its appearance. Over the temple and cheekbone it was as glazed and as shiny as varnished parchment. There was no suggestion of pores.

One could not fancy a drop of moisture upon that arid surface. From brow to chin, however, it was crosshatched by a million delicate wrinkles, which shot and interlaced as though Nature in some Maori mood had tried how wild and intricate a pattern she could devise.

"*Où est la collection de Memphis?*" asked the student, with the awkward air of a man who is devising a question merely for the purpose of opening a conversation.

"*C'est là,*" replied the man brusquely, nodding his head at the other side of the room.

"*Vous êtes un Egyptien, n'est-ce pas?*" asked the Englishman.

The attendant looked up and turned his strange dark eyes upon his questioner. They were vitreous, with a misty dry shininess, such as Smith had never seen in a human head before. As he gazed into them he saw some strong emotion gather in their depths, which rose and deepened until it broke into a look of something akin both to horror and to hatred.

"*Non, monsieur; je suis français.*" The man turned abruptly and bent low over his polishing. The student gazed at him for a moment in astonishment, then went through one of the doors. He proceeded to make notes of his researches among the papyri. His thoughts, however, refused to return into their natural groove. They would run upon the enigmatical attendant with the sphinxlike face and the parchment skin.

"Where have I seen such eyes?" said Vansittart Smith to himself. "There is something saurian about them, something reptilian. There's the *membrana nictitans* of the snakes," he mused, bethinking himself of his zoological studies. "It gives a shiny effect. But there was something more here. There was a sense of power, of wisdom—so I read them—and of weariness, utter weariness, and ineffable despair. It may be all imagination, but I never had so strong an impression. By Jove, I must have another look at them!" He rose and paced round the Egyptian rooms, but the man who had excited his curiosity had disappeared.

The student sat down again in his quiet corner and continued to work at his notes. He had gained the information which he required from the papyri, and it only remained to write it down while it was still fresh in his memory. For a time his pencil traveled rapidly over the paper, but soon the lines became less level, the words more blurred, and finally the pencil tinkled down upon the floor, and the head of the student dropped heavily forward upon his chest. Tired out by his journey, he slept so soundly in his lonely post behind the door that neither the clanking civil guard, nor the footsteps of sightseers, nor even the loud hoarse bell which gives the signal for closing, were sufficient to arouse him.

Twilight deepened into darkness, the bustle from the Rue de Rivoli waxed and then waned, distant Nôtre Dame clanged out the hour of midnight, and still the dark and lonely figure sat silently in the shadow. It was not until close upon one in the morning that with a sudden gasp and an intaking of the breath Vansittart Smith returned to consciousness. For a moment it flashed upon him that he had dropped asleep in his study chair at home. The moon was shining fitfully through the unshuttered window, however, and as his eye ran along the lines of mummies and the endless array of polished cases, he remembered clearly where he was and how he came there. The student was not a nervous man. He possessed that love of a novel situation which is peculiar to his race. Stretching out his cramped limbs, he looked at his watch and burst into a chuckle as he observed the hour. The episode would make an admirable anecdote to be introduced into his next paper as a relief to the graver and heavier speculations. He was a little cold but wide awake and much refreshed. It was no wonder that the guardians had overlooked him, for the door threw its heavy black shadow right across him.

The complete silence was impressive. Neither outside nor inside was there a creak or a murmur. He was alone with the dead men of a dead civilization. Though the outer city reeked of the garish 19th century, in all this chamber there was scarce an article, from the shriveled ear of wheat to the pigment box of the painter, which had not held its own against four thousand years. Here was the flotsam and jetsam washed up by the great ocean of time from that far-off empire. From stately Thebes, from lordly Luxor, from the great temples of Heliopolis, from a hundred rifled tombs, these relics had been brought.

The student glanced around at the long-silent figures who flickered vaguely up through the gloom, at the busy toilers who were now so restful, and he fell into a reverent and thoughtful mood. An unwonted sense of his own youth and insignificance came over him. Leaning back in his chair, he gazed dreamily down the long vista of rooms, all silvery with the moonshine, which extend through the whole wing of the widespread building. His eyes fell upon the yellow glare of a distant lamp.

John Vansittart Smith sat up on his chair with his nerves all on edge. The light was advancing slowly toward him, pausing from time to time, and then coming jerkily onward. The bearer moved noiselessly. In the utter silence there was no suspicion of the pat of a footfall. An idea of robbers entered the Englishman's head. He snuggled up farther into the corner. The light was two rooms off. Now it was in the next chamber and still there was no sound. With something approaching to a thrill of fear the student observed a face, floating in the air as it were, behind the flare of the lamp. The figure was wrapped in shadow, but the light fell full upon a strange, eager face. There was no mistaking the metallic, glistening eyes and the cadaverous skin. It was the attendant with whom he had conversed.

Vansittart Smith's first impulse was to come forward and address him. A few words of explanation would set the matter clear and lead doubtless to his being conducted to some side door from which he might make his way to his hotel. As the man entered the chamber, however, there was something so stealthy in his movements and so furtive in his expression that the Englishman altered his intention. This was clearly no ordinary official walking the rounds. The fellow wore felt-soled slippers, stepped with a rising chest, and glanced quickly from left to right, while his hurried, gasping breathing thrilled the flame of his lamp. Vansittart Smith crouched silently back into the corner and watched him keenly, convinced that his errand was one of secret and probably sinister import.

There was no hesitation in the other's movements. He stepped lightly and swiftly across to one of the great cases and, drawing a key from his pocket, he unlocked it. From the upper shelf he pulled down a mummy, which he bore away with him, and laid it with much care and solicitude upon the ground. By it he placed his lamp, and then squatting down beside it in Eastern fashion he began with long, quivering fingers to undo the grave wrappings and bandages which girt it round. As the crackling rolls of linen peeled off one after the other, a strong aromatic odor filled the chamber, and fragments of scented wood and of spices pattered down upon the marble floor.

It was clear to John Vansittart Smith that this mummy had never been unswathed before. The operation interested him keenly. He thrilled all over with curiosity, and his birdlike head protruded farther and farther from behind the door. When, however, the last roll had been removed from the four-thousand-year-old head, it was all that he could do to stifle an outcry of amazement.

First, a cascade of long, black, glossy tresses poured over the workman's hands and arms. A second turn of the bandage revealed a low, white forehead, with a pair of delicately arched eyebrows. A third uncovered a pair of bright, deeply fringed eyes, and a straight, well-cut nose, while a fourth and last showed a sweet, full, sensitive mouth, and a beautifully curved chin. The whole face was one of extraordinary loveliness, save for the one blemish that in the center of the forehead there was a single irregular, coffee-colored splotch. It was a triumph of the embalmer's art. Vansittart Smith's eyes grew larger and larger as he gazed upon it, and he chirruped in his throat with satisfaction.

Its effect upon the Egyptologist was as nothing, however, compared with that which it produced upon the strange attendant. He threw his hands up into the air, burst into a harsh clatter of words, and then, hurling himself down upon the ground beside the mummy, he threw his arms round her, and kissed her repeatedly upon the lips and brow. *"Ma petite!"* he groaned in French. *"Ma pauvre petite!"* His voice broke with emotion, and his innumerable wrinkles quivered and writhed, but the student observed in the lamplight that his shining eyes were still dry and tearless as two beads of steel. For some minutes he lay, with a twitching face, crooning and moaning over the beautiful head. Then he broke into a sudden smile, said some words in an unknown tongue, and sprang to his feet with the vigorous air of one who has braced himself for an effort.

In the center of the room there was a large, circular case which contained, as the student had frequently remarked,

a magnificent collection of early Egyptian rings and precious stones. To this the attendant strode, and, unlocking it, threw it open. On the ledge at the side he placed his lamp, and beside it a small, earthenware jar which he had drawn from his pocket. He then took a handful of rings from the case, and with a most serious and anxious face he proceeded to smear each in turn with some liquid substance from the earthen pot, holding them to the light as he did so. He was clearly disappointed with the first lot, for he threw them petulantly back into the case and drew out some more. One of these, a massive ring with a large crystal set in it, he seized and eagerly tested with the contents of the jar.

Instantly he uttered a cry of joy, and threw out his arms in a wild gesture which upset the pot and set the liquid streaming across the floor to the very feet of the Englishman. The attendant drew a red handkerchief from his bosom, and, mopping up the mess, he followed it into the corner, where in a moment he found himself face to face with his observer.

"Excuse me," said John Vansittart Smith, with all imaginable politeness; "I have been unfortunate enough to fall asleep behind this door."

"And you have been watching me?" the other asked in English, with a most venomous look on his corpselike face.

The student was a man of veracity. "I confess," said he, "that I have noticed your movements, and that they have aroused my curiosity and interest in the highest degree."

The man drew a long, flamboyant-bladed knife from his bosom. "You have had a very narrow escape," he said; "had I seen you ten minutes ago, I should have driven this through your heart. As it is, if you touch me or interfere with me in any way you are a dead man."

"I have no wish to interfere with you," the student answered. "My presence here is entirely accidental. All I ask is that you will have the extreme kindness to show me out through some side door." He spoke with great suavity, for the man was still pressing the tip of his dagger against the palm of his left hand, as though to assure himself of its sharpness, while his face preserved its malignant expression.

"If I thought—" said he. "But no, perhaps it is as well. What is your name?" The Englishman gave it.

"Vansittart Smith," the other repeated. "Are you the same Vansittart Smith who gave a paper in London upon El Kab? I saw a report of it. Your knowledge of the subject is contemptible."

"Sir!" cried the Egyptologist.

"Yet it is superior to that of many who make even greater pretensions. The whole keystone of our old life in Egypt was not the inscriptions or monuments of which you make so much, but was our hermetic philosophy and mystic knowledge of which you say little or nothing."

"Our old life!" repeated the scholar, wide-eyed; and then suddenly, "Good God, look at the mummy's face!"

The strange man turned and flashed his light upon the dead woman, uttering a long, doleful cry as he did so. The action of the air had already undone all the art of the embalmer. The skin had fallen away, the eyes had sunk inward, the discolored lips had writhed away from the yellow teeth, and the brown mark upon the forehead alone showed that it was indeed the same face which had shown such youth and beauty a few short minutes before.

The man flapped his hands together in grief and horror. Then mastering himself by a strong effort he turned his hard eyes once more upon the Englishman.

"It does not matter," he said, in a shaking voice. "It really does not matter. I came here tonight with the fixed determination to do something. It is now done. All else is as nothing. I have found my quest. The old curse is broken. I can rejoin her. What matter about her inanimate shell so long as her spirit is awaiting me at the other side of the veil!"

"These are wild words," said Vansittart Smith. He was becoming more and more convinced that he had to do with a madman.

"Time presses, and I must go," continued the other. "The moment is at hand for which I have waited this weary time. But I must show you out first. Come with me."

Taking up the lamp, he turned from the disordered chamber, and led the student swiftly through the long series of the Egyptian, Assyrian, and Persian apartments. At the end of the latter he pushed open a small door let into the wall and descended a winding, stone stair. The Englishman felt the cold, fresh air of the night upon his brow. There was a door opposite him which appeared to communicate with the street. To the right of this another door stood ajar, throwing a spurt of yellow light across the passage. "Come in here!" said the attendant shortly.

Vansittart Smith hesitated. He had hoped that he had come to the end of his adventure. Yet his curiosity was strong within him. He could not leave the matter unsolved, so he followed his strange companion into the lighted chamber.

It was a small room, such as is devoted to a concierge. A wood fire sparkled in the grate. At one side stood a truckle bed, and at the other a coarse, wooden chair, with a round table in the center, which bore the remains of a meal. As the visitor's eye glanced round he could not but remark with an ever-recurring thrill that all the small details of the room were of the most quaint design and antique workmanship. The candlesticks, the vases upon the chimney piece, the fire irons, the ornaments upon the walls, were all such as he had been wont to associate with the remote past. The gnarled, heavy-eyed man sat himself down upon the edge of the bed, and motioned his guest into the chair.

"There may be design in this," he said, still speaking excellent English. "It may be decreed that I should leave some account behind as a warning to all rash mortals who would set their wits up against workings of nature. I leave it with you. Make such use as you will of it. I speak to you now with my feet upon the threshold of the other world.

"I am, as you surmised, an Egyptian—not one of the downtrodden race of slaves who now inhabit the delta of the Nile, but a survivor of that fiercer and harder people who tamed the Hebrew, drove the Ethiopian back into the southern deserts, and built those mighty works which have been the envy and the wonder of all after generations. It was in the reign of Tuthmosis, 1,600 years before the birth of Christ, that I first saw the light. You shrink away from me. Wait, and you will see that I am more to be pitied than to be feared.

"My name was Sosra. My father had been the chief priest of Osiris in the great temple of Abaris, which stood in those days upon the Bubastic branch of the Nile. I was brought up in the temple and was trained in all those mystic arts which are spoken of in your own Bible. I was an apt pupil. Before I was 16 I had learned all which the wisest priest could teach me. From that time on I studied nature's secrets for myself, and shared my knowledge with no man.

"Of all the questions which attracted me there were none over which I labored so long as over those which concern themselves with the nature of life. I probed deeply into the vital principle. The aim of medicine had been to drive away disease when it appeared. It seemed to me that a method might be devised which should so fortify the body as to prevent weakness or death from ever taking hold of it. It is useless that I should recount my researches. You would scarce comprehend them if I did. They were carried out partly upon animals, partly upon slaves, and partly on myself.

"Suffice it that their result was to furnish me with a substance which, when injected into the blood, would endow the body with strength to resist the effects of time, of violence, or of disease. It would not indeed confer immortality, but its potency would endure for many thousands of years. I used it upon a cat, and afterward drugged the creature with the most deadly poisons. That cat is alive in Lower Egypt at the present moment. There was nothing of mystery or magic in the matter. It was simply a chemical discovery, which may well be made again.

"Love of life runs high in the young. It seemed to me that I had broken away from all human care now that I had abolished pain and driven death to such a distance. With a light heart I poured the accursed stuff into my veins. Then I looked round for someone whom I could benefit. There was a young priest of Thoth, Parmes by name, who had won my goodwill by his earnest nature and his devotion to his studies. To him I whispered my secret, and at his request I injected him with my elixir. I should now, I reflected, never be without a companion of the same age as myself.

"After this grand discovery I relaxed my studies to some extent, but Parmes continued his with redoubled energy. Every day I could see him working with his flasks and his distiller in the Temple of Thoth, but he said little to me as to the result of his labors. For my own part, I used to walk through the city and look around me with exultation as I reflected that all this was destined to pass away and that only I should remain. The people would bow to me as they passed me, for the fame of my knowledge had gone abroad.

"There was war at this time, and the Great King had sent down his soldiers to the eastern boundary to drive away the Hyksos. A governor, too, was sent to Abaris, that he might hold it for the king. I had heard much of the beauty of the daughter of this governor, but one day as I walked out with Parmes we met her, borne upon the shoulders of her slaves. I was struck with love as with lightning. My heart went out from me. I could have thrown myself beneath the feet of her bearers. This was my woman. Life without her was impossible. I swore by the head of Horus that she should be mine. I swore it to the priest of Thoth. He turned away from me with a brow which was as black as midnight.

There is no need to tell you of our wooing. She came to love me even as I loved her. I learned that Parmes had seen her before I did, and had shown her that he, too, loved her, but I could smile at his passion for I knew that her heart was mine. The white plague had come upon the city and many were stricken, but I laid my hands upon the sick and nursed them without fear or scathe. She marveled at my daring. Then I told her my secret and begged her that she would let me use my art upon her.

" 'Your flower shall then be unwithered, Atma,' I said. 'Other things may pass away, but you, and I, and our great love for each other shall outlive the tomb of King Chefru.'

"But she was full of timid, maidenly objections. 'Was it right?' she asked, 'was it not a thwarting of the will of the gods? If the great Osiris had wished that our years should be so long, would he not himself have brought it about?'

"With fond and loving words I overcame her doubts, and yet she hesitated. It was a great question, she said. She would think it over for this one night. In the morning I should know of her resolution. Surely one night was not too much to ask.

"She wished to pray to Isis for help in her decision.

"With a sinking heart and a sad foreboding of evil I left her with her tirewomen. In the morning, when the early sacrifice was over, I hurried to her house. A frightened slave met me upon the steps. Her mistress was ill, she said, very ill. In a frenzy I broke my way through the attendants, and rushed through hall and corridor to my Atma's chamber. She lay upon her couch, her head high upon the pillow, with a pallid face and glazed eye. On her forehead there blazed a single angry, purple patch. I knew that hell mark of old. It was the scar of the white plague, the sign manual of death.

"Why should I speak of that terrible time? For months I was mad, fevered, delirious, and yet I could not die. Never did an Arab thirst after the sweet wells as I longed after death. Could poison or steel have shortened the thread of my existence, I should soon have rejoined my love in the land with the narrow portal. I tried, but it was of no avail. The accursed influence was too strong upon me. One night as I lay upon my couch, weak and weary, Parmes, the priest of Thoth, came to my chamber. He stood in the circle of the lamplight, and he looked down upon me with eyes which were bright with a mad joy.

" 'Why did you let the maiden die?' he asked; 'why did you not strengthen her as you strengthened me?'

" 'I was too late,' I answered. 'But I had forgot. You also loved her. You are my fellow in misfortune. Is it not terrible to think of the centuries which must pass ere we look upon her again? Fools, fools, that we were to take death to be our enemy!'

" 'You may say that,' he cried with a wild laugh; 'The words come well from your lips. For me they have no meaning.'

" 'What mean you?' I cried, raising myself upon my elbow. 'Surely, friend, this grief has turned your brain.' His face was aflame with joy, and he writhed and shook like one who hath a devil.

"'Do you know whither I go?' he asked.

"'Nay,' I answered, 'I cannot tell.'

"'I go to her,' said he. 'she lies embalmed in the farther tomb by the double palm tree beyond the city wall.'

"'Why do you go there?' I cried.

"'To die!' he shrieked, 'to die! I am not bound by earthen fetters.'

"'But the elixir is in your blood,' I cried.

"'I can defy it,' said he; 'I have found a stronger principle which will destroy it. It is working in my veins at this moment, and in an hour I shall be a dead man. I shall join her, and you shall remain behind.'

"As I looked upon him I could see that he spoke words of truth. The light in his eye told me that he was indeed beyond the power of the elixir.

"'You will teach me!' I cried.

"'Never!' he answered.

"'I implore you, by the wisdom of Thoth, by the majesty of Anubis!'

"'It is useless,' he said coldly.

"'Then I will find it out,' I cried.

"'You cannot,' he answered; 'it came to me by chance. There is one ingredient which you can never get. Save that which is in the ring of Thoth, none will ever more be made.'

"'In the ring of Thoth!' I repeated, 'where then is the ring of Thoth?'

"'That also you shall never know,' he answered. 'You won her love. Who has won in the end? I leave you to your sordid earth life. My chains are broken. I must go!' He turned upon his heel and fled from the chamber. In the morning came the news that the priest of Thoth was dead.

"My days after that were spent in study. I must find this subtle poison which was strong enough to undo the elixir. From early dawn to midnight I bent over the test tube and the furnace. Above all, I collected the papyri and the chemical flasks of the priest of Thoth. Alas! they taught me little. Here and there some hint or stray expression would raise hope in my bosom, but no good ever came of it. Still month after month I struggled on. When my heart grew faint, I would make my way to the tomb by the palm trees. There, standing by the dead casket from which the jewel had been rifled, I would feel her sweet presence and would whisper to her that I would rejoin her if mortal wit could solve the riddle.

"Parmes had said that his discovery was connected with the ring of Thoth. I had some remembrance of the trinket. It was a large and weighty circlet made, not of gold, but of a rarer and heavier metal brought from the mines of Mount Harbal. Platinum you call it. The ring had, I remembered, a hollow crystal set in it in which some few drops of liquid might be stored. Now, the secret of Parmes could not have to do with the metal alone, for there were many rings of that metal in the temple. Was it not more likely that he had stored his precious poison within the cavity of the crystal? I had scarce come to this conclusion before, in hunting through his papers, I came upon one which told me that it was indeed so and that there was still some of the liquid unused.

"But how to find the ring? It was not upon him when he was stripped for the embalmer. Of that I made sure. Neither was it among his private effects. In vain I searched every room that he had entered, every box and vase and chattel that he had owned. I sifted the very sand of the desert in places where he had been wont to walk; but, do what I would, I could come upon no traces of the ring of Thoth. Yet it may be that I could have overcome all obstacles had it not been for a new and unlooked for misfortune.

"A great war had been waged against the Hyksos, and the captains of the Great King had been cut off in the desert, with all their bowmen and horsemen. The shepherd tribes were upon us like the locusts in a dry year. From the wilderness of Shur to the great, bitter lake there was blood by day and fire by night. Abaris was the bulwark of Egypt, but we could not keep the savages back. The city fell. The governor and the soldiers were put to the sword and I, with many more, was led away into captivity.

"For years and years I tended cattle in the great plains by the Euphrates. My master died and his son grew old, but I was still as far from death as ever. At last I escaped upon a swift camel and made my way back to Egypt. The Hyksos had settled in the land which they had conquered, and their own king ruled over the country. Abaris had been torn down, the city had been burned, and of the great temple there was nothing left save an unsightly mound. Everywhere the tombs had been rifled and the monuments destroyed. Of my Atma's grave no sign was left. It was buried in the sands of the desert, and the palm trees which marked the spot had long disappeared. The papers of Parmes and the remains of the temple of Thoth were either destroyed or scattered far and wide over the deserts of Syria. All search after them was vain.

"From that time I gave up all hope of ever finding the ring or discovering the subtle drug. I set myself to live as patiently as might be until the effect of the elixir should wear away. How can you understand how terrible a thing time is, you who have experience only of the narrow course which lies between the cradle and the grave! I know it to my cost, I who have floated down the whole stream of history. I was old when Herodotus came to Memphis. I was bowed down with years when the new gospel came upon earth. Yet you see me much as other men are, with the cursed elixir still sweetening my blood, and guarding me against that which I would court. Now, at last, at last I have come to the end of it!

"I have traveled in all lands and I have dwelt with all nations. Every tongue is the same to me. I learned them all to help pass the weary time. I need not tell you how slowly they drifted by, the long dawn of modern civilization, the dreary middle years, the dark times of barbarism. They are all behind me now. I have never looked with the eyes of love upon another woman. Atma knows that I have been constant to her.

"It was my custom to read all that the scholars had to say upon ancient Egypt. I have been in many positions, sometimes affluent, sometimes poor, but I have always found enough to enable me to buy the journals which deal with such matters. Some nine months ago I was in San Francisco, when I read an account of some discoveries made in the neighborhood of Abaris.

"My heart leapt into my mouth as I read it. It said that the excavator had busied himself in exploring some tombs recently unearthed. In one there had been found an unopened mummy with an inscription upon the outer case setting forth that it contained the body of the daughter of the governor of the city in the days of Tuthmosis. It added that on removing the outer case there had been exposed a large platinum ring set with a crystal, which had been laid upon the breast of the embalmed woman. This, then, was where Parmes had hid the ring of Thoth. He might well say that it was safe, for no Egyptian would ever stain his soul by moving even the outer case of a buried friend.

"That very night I set off from San Francisco and in a few weeks I found myself once more at Abaris, if a few sand heaps and crumbling walls may retain the name of the great city. I hurried to the Frenchmen who were digging there and asked them for the ring. They replied that both the ring and the mummy had been sent to the Boulak Museum at Cairo. To Boulak I went, but only to be told that Mariette Bey had claimed them and had shipped them to the Louvre. I followed them and there, and at last, in the Egyptian chamber I came, after close upon four thousand years, upon the remains of my Atma and upon the ring for which I had sought so long.

"But how was I to lay hands upon them? How was I to have them for my very own? It chanced that the office of attendant was vacant. I went to the director. I convinced him that I knew much about Egypt. In my eagerness I said too much. He remarked that a professor's chair would suit me better than a seat in the conciergerie. I knew more, he said, than he did. It was only by blundering and letting him think that he had overestimated my knowledge that I prevailed upon him to let me move the few effects which I have retained into this chamber. It is my first and my last night here.

"Such is my story, Mr. Vansittart Smith. I need not say more to a man of your perception. By a strange chance you have this night looked upon the face of the woman whom I loved in those far-off days. There were many rings with crystals in the case, and I had to test for the platinum to be sure of the one which I wanted. A glance at the crystal has shown me that the liquid is indeed within it, and that I shall at last be able to shake off that accursed health which has been worse to me than the foulest disease. I have nothing more to say to you. I have unburdened myself. You may tell my story or you may withhold it at your pleasure. The choice rests with you. I owe you some amends, for you have had a narrow escape of your life this night. I was a desperate man, and not to be balked in my purpose. Had I seen you before the thing was done, I might have put it beyond your power to oppose me or to raise an alarm. This is the door. It leads into the Rue de Rivoli. Good night."

The Englishman glanced back. For a moment the lean figure of Sosra the Egyptian stood framed in the narrow doorway. The next the door had slammed, and the heavy rasping of the bolt broke on the silent night.

It was on the second day after his return to London that Mr. John Vansittart Smith saw the following concise narrative in the Paris correspondence of the *Times*:

—CURIOUS OCCURRENCE IN THE LOUVRE—
Yesterday morning a strange discovery was made in the principal Eastern chamber. The *ouvriers* who are employed to clean out the rooms in the morning found one of the attendants lying dead upon the floor with his arms around one of the mummies. So close was his embrace that it was only with the utmost difficulty that they were separated.

One of the cases containing valuable rings had been opened and rifled. The authorities are of opinion that the man was bearing away the mummy with some idea of selling it to a private collector, but that he was struck down in the very act by long-standing disease of the heart. It is said that he was a man of uncertain age and eccentric habits, without any living relations to mourn over his dramatic and untimely end.

GLOSSARY

Abaris - Ancient priest of Apollo. According to legend, Apollo gave
   Abaris a golden arrow which he could use to ride through the
   air. It made him invisible, cured diseases, and gave oracles.

À la bonheur! - French for "What luck!"

Anubis - Ancient Egyptian god of the dead and of mummification,
   usually depicted as having the body of a man and the head
   of a jackal.

apathy - Lack of emotion, concern, or feeling.

Arcadian - Arcadia was an area in Greece where people supposedly
   lived simple, contented lives as farmers and shepherds. An
   Arcadian lifestyle is rustic, innocent, and pastoral.

ardor - Enthusiasm.

athwart - Across, in opposition to.

banns - A church announcement of an intended marriage.

bereavement - The state or fact of being desolate or alone after the
   death of someone close.

bier - A stand on which a corpse or coffin is placed.

blackleading - A type of black polish made from graphite and used on
   stoves, fire irons, and other iron surfaces that got hot.

boudoir - Bedroom or dressing room.

bromide of potassium - A mineral salt given as a sedative (a sleep-
   inducing medicine).

Bubastic branch of the Nile - A branch of the Nile River that flowed
   past the ancient city of Bubastis (now Tell Basta), north of Cairo.

cairn - A heap of stones piled up as a memorial or as a landmark.

calcined - Heating something to a high temperature below the
   melting or fusing point, causing loss of moisture, oxidation,
   and decomposition.

capricious - Unpredictable.

C'est là - French for "It's over there."

Champollion - Jean François Champollion, a French Egyptologist
   in the early years of the 19th century who was the first to

correctly decipher Egyptian hieroglyphics by using the newly discovered Rosetta Stone. This stone had a message written in hieroglyphics, demotic writing, and Greek. Champollion used the Greek portion as a key to translating the other forms of writing.

the Channel - The English Channel, between England and France.

Chippendale - Furniture designed by Thomas Chippendale, an 18th century furniture designer; furniture that copies the Chippendale style.

chirruped - Chirped.

concierge - In France, a person who lives in an apartment house or other building, looks after the entrance, and cleans up.

conjecture - Conclusion based on guesswork.

coppices - Thickets, groves, forests.

coquetted - Flirted.

covetous - Greedy.

cuirass - Armor plating.

Demotic - A simplified form of Egyptian writing.

Dieppe - A seaport on the northern coast of France.

digress - To leave the main topic.

dionine - (herodionine) A drug which, in addition to poisoning dogs in ghost stories, is used in combination with other substances to treat eye infections.

dolorosa - An expression usually used in music meaning soft and pathetic. **Via dolorosa** is a sad life.

dowered - Given to, as in a gift.

dross - Scum that forms on the surface of molten metal.

endearments - Expressions of affection.

enigmatical - Mysterious.

expiation - The act of making amends.

exultation - Joy.

fidelity - Faithfulness.

flotsam and jetsam - Cargo and wreckage from wrecked ships. Flotsam is still afloat, jetsam has been washed ashore.

funk - Cowardly fright or panic.

gibbering - Chattering.

girt - Encircle.

glebe - Cultivable land owned by a church.

gratis - Free, without charge.

gravity - As it is used in Bierce's story, it means seriousness.

greatcoat - A heavy overcoat. In Victorian times, a greatcoat often had capes over the shoulders.

guinea - A British coin worth 21 shillings, 1 shilling more than a pound.

Heliopolis - An ancient city northeast of Cairo, Egypt. Heliopolis (Greek for "City of the Sun") was the center of worship for the Egyptian sun god, Ra Horakhty.

hermetic - Relating to the Gnostic writings or teachings arising in the first three centuries A.D. and attributed to Hermes Trismegistus

Hollands - Gin.

île de la Grenouillière - Frog Island.

intimations - Hints.

Isis - Ancient Egyptian goddess who possessed the virtues of wife and mother and protected the dead.

Jaunting car - *Jaunt* refers to a short, fun trip. Probably an automobile for taking short pleasure trips. (See comments accompanying *pigging it.*)

Lepsius - Karl Lepsius, a German Egyptologist of the middle 19th century. Lepsius helped unearth the Egyptian city of Tanis and discovered a stone engraved with hieroglyphics and several other forms of writing, including ancient Greek. Using the Greek as a key, Lepsius translated the stone document, known now as the Degree of Canopus. Several decades earlier, **Champollion** translated the Rosetta Stone in a similar fashion.

Louvre - Now the largest museum of art in the world, located in Paris. The Louvre was originally a fortress built by Philippe Auguste in the 13th century, and was later rebuilt and restyled to become the royal palace. As early as 1747, rooms were set aside for art students to view the royal art collection. In addition to such treasures as the Mona Lisa and the Venus de Milo, the Louvre also houses an extensive collection of Egyptian artifacts.

Luxor - A village in Egypt, once the site of the ancient capital of **Thebes**.

magnum opus - A great work or masterpiece, used especially when referring to literature or art.

mahlstick - A stick painters use to brace their hand on so as not to touch the wet paint of their canvas.

malevolent - Having a wicked or harmful influence.

Maori - Native people of New Zealand. Maori warriors often tattooed their faces with complex designs.

Ma petite! Ma pauvre petite! - French: Literally, "My little one! My poor little one!" Used this way, *petite* can be a word of endearment, like *sweetheart*.

Mariette Bey - Edouard Auguste Mariette, 19th century French archaeologist who discovered the famous giant stone carvings of the sacred bull, Apis, in Memphis, Egypt. The bulls are now on display at the **Louvre**. The "Bey" in this name is an honorary title given to Egyptian dignitaries.

melancholy - Sad, gloomy, depressed.

membrana nictitans - Nictitating membrane, the membrane under the eyelid of many animals.

Mesmer - An 18th century Austrian physician who used magnets, which were poorly understood at the time, in an attempt to cure patients. Mesmer believed that stars and living beings, as well as iron, had magnetic qualities. He also discovered what we now call hypnotism, which was first called "mesmerism," from which we get the word *mesmerized*.

morbid - Gruesome, deathly.

morion - A kind of helmet with peaked brim running front to rear over the center of the head.

mutable - Changeable.

Non, monsieur; je suis français - French: "No, sir, I'm French."

Norsemen - The Vikings.

Nôtre Dame - The great cathedral of Paris, built between 1163 and 1345.

occult - Literally, this word means "hidden," which is how the word is used in the story "Man-sized in Marble."

Osiris - Ancient Egyptian god of fertility and eternal life after death, usually depicted as a mummy with a pharaoh's crown.

ostentatious - Boastful, showy.

Où est la collection de Memphis? - French: "Where is the collection of Memphis (Egypt)?" The speaker wishes to see a collection of Egyptian artifacts.

ouvriers - French for laborer, workman.

Palais Royal - Literally, "royal palace." The Palais Royal in Paris was originally built as the home of Cardinal Richelieu, minister to Louis XIII. It later became the residence of the royal family.

pallor and fixity - Pale and unmoving.

papyri - Plural of *papyrus*, referring both to the paperlike material Egyptians made from reeds and to the scrolls of papyrus they wrote on.

penance - To show sorrow for past wrongdoing.

pentacle - A five-pointed star formed by five straight lines connecting the points of a pentagon while maintaining the pentagon's outline, usually drawn on the floor in chalk and believed by some to be useful in protecting one against evil spirits.

phantasmagoria - Things which seem fantastic, dreamlike.

pigging it - From the context of the sentence ("he was **pigging it** there with his boy brother and another American") the phrase appears to mean: living without much outside help. We might say "batching it" from the word bachelor. It is not a term we use today and perhaps never was. Since the character who uses it in Hodgson's story is an American, and Hodgson was not, it may be that Hodgson didn't exactly know how Americans spoke and made up phrases he hoped would sound like American slang to his fellow English readers. (See also *scratch feed* and *jaunting car*.)

poignant - Painful.

preeminence - Superior, outstanding.

privation - Lack of the basic necessities.

race - At the time these stories were written, *race* usually referred to ethnic groups rather than people of different physical characteristics.

respite - Relief.

reticulated - Netlike. **Reticulated windows** are made up of many small diamond-shaped panes.

Rubinstein - Anton Rubinstein, a Russian pianist and composer of the 19th century.

Rue de Rivoli - The street that runs along the north wing (the Richelieu wing) of the Louvre.

GLOSSARY

saurian - Lizardlike.

scratch feed - Probably refers to a quickly fixed meal. (See comments accompanying *pigging it*.)

screw - Victorian slang term for money. "Perhaps she wants a rise in her screw," means she wants higher wages.

Seine - A major river in France that flows through the heart of Paris.

somnambulist - A sleepwalker.

spinet - Small upright piano.

stucco - A plasterlike finish made of cement and sand for the exterior walls of a house.

sweetmeats - Candy or dried fruits.

taciturn - Quiet, untalkative.

tessellated - A mosaic pattern.

tête-à-tête - French for "head to head," meaning a private conversation between two people.

Thebes - Capital of ancient Egypt around 2000 B.C. Now consists of the villages of **Luxor** and Karnak.

Thoth - Ancient Egyptian god of wisdom and writing, usually depicted as having the body of a human and the head of an ibis (a storklike bird).

tirewomen - Old-fashioned word for lady's maids.

truckle bed - A low bed on small wheels that can be pushed under a larger bed. Also called a trundle bed.

Tuthmosis - Name taken by at least four pharaohs of ancient Egypt during the 18th Dynasty (between 1570 and 1293 B.C).

the veil - A poetic term for the separation between the world of the living and the world of the dead. **At the other side of the veil** is a euphemism for death.

vesta - Match made of wood or wax named for the Roman goddess of the hearth.

vitreous - Glassy.

Vous êtes un Egyptien, n'est-ce pas? French: "You're an Egyptian, isn't that so?"

vulgar - Crude.

Whately - Richard Whately, an 18th century philosopher and rhetorician.